AURORA
S C H O O L

DATE DUE

JA 57 '05			

The Kingfisher's Gift

The *Kingfisher's* *Gift*

SUSAN WILLIAMS BECKHORN

Philomel Books ⌣ New York

Library of Congress Cataloging-in-Publication Data
Beckhorn, Susan Williams, 1953–
The kingfisher's gift / Susan Williams Beckhorn.
p.   cm.   Summary: After the sudden death
of her beloved father, twelve-year-old Franny spends the summer
with her unique paternal grandmother in Wayland, Massachusetts,
where she continues to care for the fairies her father knew as a boy
while at the same time wrestling with her own grief
as well as the old and new griefs of her mother and grandmother.
[1. Fairies—Fiction. 2. Grief—Fiction. 3. Fathers and daughters—Fiction. 4. Mothers and
daughters—Fiction. 5. Grandmothers—Fiction. 6. Wayland (Mass.)—Fiction.] I. Title.
PZ7.B381735 Ki 2002   [Fic]—dc21   2001051348
ISBN 0-399-23712-7
1 3 5 7 9 10 8 6 4 2
First Impression

To my mother and father,
Mary Lou and Wally Williams,
who gave me a childhood
of stories, nature, and imagination.

I'd also like to express my gratitude to
Michael Green and Patti Gauch:
editors extraordinaire, teachers, and friends.
This story is partly theirs.

Chapter One ⁓

"WHAT'S IN THE BASKET, MISSY?"

Franny knew that even those few words were an effort for Henry, squeezed out because he felt sorry for her. "Nothing," she whispered, trying to avoid his eyes. Henry was Grandmother Morrow's chauffeur. She saw him give her a puzzled look as he opened the door of the car for her.

Franny did not turn her head to look at Mama, or her grandparents Nana and Baba. She was being sent to stay with her other grandmother, Grandmother Morrow, the one they didn't like, for the rest of the spring and the entire summer. Nana and Baba were taking Mama to Europe on the steamer *Olympic*, which sailed tomorrow at dawn. Nana stooped down, with a rustle of black silk, and hissed in her ear, "You could at least say good-bye to your mother. You won't be seeing her for four months, and after all, her breakdown is as much because of your willfully perverse behavior as it is your papa's death." Franny glanced up. There was anger, like blue sparks, in Nana's eyes.

But Franny couldn't say good-bye. After what Mama had done, it didn't seem like there was anything to say to her ever again.

"Now, don't you worry about us," Baba said kindly to Franny. "There are plenty of lifeboats, it's a good, stout ship, and it's hardly her maiden voyage." He bent and gave her a kiss. Franny knew he was trying to get her to smile. But she wouldn't smile and she wasn't worrying about their voyage.

She was thinking about the flurry of packing, through which Mama sat as if she were wrapped in an invisible blanket of silence. She remembered watching Nana inspecting Mama's tea dresses and ball gowns, which had been hidden in her closet for the last six months, Nana directing the packing of gloves, jewelry, and other small things. "Elizabeth, what you need is rest and a complete change," Nana had announced to Franny's mother—and so they were going, leaving Franny behind.

Now Nana took Franny's chin in her hand and made her turn her head to them. "It is to be hoped you will get ahold of yourself in Wayland and stop this ridiculous fantasizing." Franny slid her eyes sideways to glance at Mama, but Mama's eyes seemed to stare at the ground. Neither of them said anything.

Franny felt herself looking right through Nana. She hugged the basket tighter to her chest. Then, abruptly, she twisted away and climbed into the gleaming black automobile.

The car had belonged to Grandfather Morrow. Franny

remembered the quiet man with the shaggy moustache who had loved to drive his big, shiny car. He employed Henry to drive his wife, to keep the vehicle in tip-top running order, and as a handyman around the place, but Grandfather preferred to do his own driving. Grandmother kept the car after his death, but she never learned to drive.

Now Henry started up the engine and pulled away from the curb. He didn't even have to turn a crank at the front, because Grandmother Morrow's car was a Cadillac Touring Car with an electric starter. Henry was tall, and thin as a string. He had to fold himself up to fit in the driver's seat, and his head nearly brushed the roof. He looked straight ahead as he drove, and said nothing. That was more like the man Franny remembered.

"He's not unfriendly," Papa had told her once. "He's just a country boy who never learned how to converse, except with trout and automobile engines."

"Why do you call Henry a boy, Papa? He's all grown up."

"That's just an expression, Franny. You're right, he's certainly not a boy, though a man just past thirty is far from old. Poor fellow, he took it hard when his wife died."

"He still thinks about her," Franny had said to Papa then. "I can tell by his eyes. That's what makes him seem old."

Still refusing to look behind her, Franny leaned back on the leather seat, smelling its dusty, travelly smell. Her fingers gripped the handle of the little wicker basket at the thought of Papa. She winced and held it more carefully in her lap—carefully because her hands were bandaged and still hurt so much, and carefully because of what was inside.

Franny gazed out the open window at Mount Auburn Street. It was dappled with the shadows of big elms, dressed now in the tender green of late spring. The lilacs that had bloomed in nearly every yard a few weeks ago were faded now, but here and there the bud of an early rose on a wall or trellis was beginning to open. They looked to Franny like the tiny pink cheeks of Aunt Florence's new baby, Georgie.

Henry slowed the car as he overtook the green milk wagon stopped in front of the Van Reusen house. The old horse was dozing, resting a hind leg, enjoying the patch of morning sun that spilled across her dusty hindquarters. Franny turned her head to look, but the mare didn't even open an eye as they passed. After a bit, the car turned onto the Boston Post Road, heading out toward Wayland.

Stiffly, Franny opened the lid of the basket and peered inside. Meadowsweet leapt to her feet when she saw Franny's face and scampered up the inner wall of the basket, using the strands of wicker for hand- and toeholds.

"Where are your shoes?" Franny whispered with a giggle.

Meadowsweet pointed a foot, wriggling her tiny toes, and indicated two scraps of brown leather that might easily have been mistaken for some sort of seed husks that had been tossed carelessly beside her mullein leaf lap robe. "Down there. Can't climb right in 'em," she explained, the corners of her mouth turning up irresistibly. She gave her daylily skirt an

4

impatient hitch with one hand and peeked over the rim of the basket, looking around at the interior of the car curiously. "Are we almost there?"

"No, silly, we just started." Franny saw that Meadowsweet's papa, King Tamarack, was lying peacefully on his back on the neatly folded tea towel that lined the bottom of the basket. His head was pillowed on his arms, one knee crossed over the other, and he was snoring softly. He looked quite natty in his white linen coat, tailored from one of Franny's papa's handkerchiefs. Around his neck he wore a fine white lambs' wool scarf that his wife, Queen Iris, had knit for him on a pair of straight pins. Franny grinned. Meadowsweet's papa never could stay awake in a car, but her mama smiled regally up at Franny from her seat on a lavender sachet borrowed from Nana's underwear drawer. She looked her usual elegant self in a traveling gown of spider's silk, dyed pale green, and a short milkweed down cape. A matching cap sat on hair like golden moonlight, and against it her delicate antennae curved like a pair of decorative feathers.

"Are you comfy?" Franny whispered.

Iris gave her husband a tiny kick. "Franny's asking if we're comfortable, love."

Tamarack opened one eye, and shifted into a more luxurious position. He could just stretch out full length in the basket. "It's a dandy way to travel. I'm glad you thought of it, youngster," he said to Franny.

"It does quite nicely," added Iris, but Meadowsweet

dropped back down to sit beside her parents with an almost soundless thump, her mood shifting like moonlight on a bead of dew. She kicked her feet and folded her arms crossly.

"I still think we should have flown to Wayland. I'm not too big. You and Papa could have flown me. It would have been so exciting."

"Now, Meadowsweet, we went all through that. You know what traveling does to my wings—dust and rain and all. Flying might be all right for common folk, but really, this is a much more suitable means of getting there."

Franny knew the real reason Iris wouldn't fly: Meadowsweet couldn't, and she was, indeed, getting too big for her parents to "fly" her by holding her by the hands between them. Meadowsweet was a changeling, a water sprite, and not a fairy child at all. It was a fact Franny had learned from Papa before he had gone away, before she knew about words like *pneumonia*, back when the Tamarack family existed only in the stories Papa told her every night before bed.

"Don't fret, 'Sweet," soothed Tamarack, opening one eye again. "Mayhap we'll find the kingfisher's feather in Wayland and all will be right." Meadowsweet pouted momentarily, but then she brightened, winking up at Franny, her slanting, blue-green eyes laughing, her wispy black curls tumbling wildly about her pointy little face. Franny laughed out loud, then caught herself, and glanced up to see Henry's eyes in the rearview mirror, giving her a positively worried look. Softly, she closed the cover of the basket.

Franny thought about Grandmother Morrow and felt her stomach rise into her chest all by itself. She knew why her DiCrista grandparents didn't like Grandmother Morrow. It was partly because she was Southern. Nana DiCrista's father had starved to death in a Confederate prison camp. There was always a sound in Nana's voice, like chewing on carelessly picked nut meats, when she talked about Franny's other grandmother. "She may have been the belle of Knoxville indeed to catch a wealthy Boston lumberman," Nana sputtered on the few occasions she mentioned Grandmother Morrow, "but she needn't offend people by insisting on calling it the War of Yankee Aggression and dragging that defeated rascal General Lee up north with her." By that Nana meant the portrait in oils of General Robert E. Lee that hung in Grandmother Morrow's living room opposite a painting of the Great Smoky Mountains.

"Now, Mama," Franny's mother would soothe, "you know the Southern army was nothing more than shoeless skeletons in rags themselves by then. How could a starving army feed prisoners as well?"

But Nana only sniffed. "It isn't just that she's Southern, Elizabeth. You must admit yourself that your mother-in-law is an eccentric naturalist. Why, she collects every dead thing under the sun. Everywhere you look in that big, gloomy house there's something dead: stuffed birds, pressed flowers, fossils, seashells, even bugs."

Franny's mother frowned then and twisted the bracelet on one slim wrist. "I have thought sometimes that she doesn't like little girls. She seems so remote when Franny's around. Perhaps, after raising three sons, two of whom produced only sons, she doesn't know what to do with a granddaughter."

"Well, it was all right when Arthur's father was living, but since he passed away, the woman's gone undeniably queer. She'd probably let Franny run barefoot, with a butterfly net in her hand, if it were up to her." Nana had looked meaningfully in Franny's direction and Franny remembered feeling uncomfortable when they talked in front of her like that.

Secretly, Franny rather liked the idea of chasing butterflies barefoot. But still, it made her heart thump strangely now, to think that after all that talk, they were sending her to spend the summer alone with Grandmother Morrow. Once, on one of their few visits together to see his mother, Papa had said, "Don't be frightened of her, Franny. Grandmother may act like a snow queen, but really, she has a very soft heart. You should see her holding a baby bird. I think something in life hurt her once. She doesn't talk about it."

All in all, it had seemed very odd to Franny when Nana announced that she should be sent to Grandmother Morrow's for the summer. But Aunt Florence wasn't well yet after Georgie's birth, at least not well enough to take on an extra child for four months, and Uncle Edward was a widower, his sons nearly grown, so there really had been no other choice. . . .

Shaking off her thoughts, Franny gazed out the window at the countryside hurtling by. When she looked back, everything behind them was screened by a cloud of brown dust. They were well out of Cambridge now. A little boy in knickers, shirttails flying, was pounding pell-mell after his hoop in the middle of the road ahead. Henry sounded the horn, and the boy stumbled in a panic. He was sitting by the ditch, rubbing his knee, staring at the car, when they passed.

At a farmhouse, a black and white collie ran out barking. He raced them, tongue hanging, grinning like mad, until they came to a bridge over a little stream. Then he stopped suddenly, and Franny, looking out the back window, watched him padding back along the dusty road to his home.

The car rumbled steadily over the ruts. It wasn't as jouncy as riding in a carriage behind a horse, but it was somehow more alone, almost as if they were the ones who were still, and it was the world that was chugging so swiftly by. Franny pulled off her hat, shut her eyes, and rested her head on the seat back, remembering. She could hear Papa's voice as if he were right there beside her. He could tell a story almost as if he were reading out of a book. It was her favorite story, the one about the fairy family, King Tamarack of the Larch World, Queen Iris, and their beautiful daughter, Princess Meadowsweet. . . .

Chapter Two ⌇

. . . Apart from his wife and daughter, Tamarack's greatest treasure was his sword. It was needle sharp, the edge honed like a razor. It had been wrought from the dorsal barb of the huge hornpout that was vanquished on that very beach where he now stood. You remember?

How could Franny forget the battle with the monster hornpout? The fish, with its gaping mouth and strange, catlike whiskers, had threatened to drag Tamarack's raft right under the dark waters of the cove, but his ally, the kingfisher bird, who could pass from air to the water realm, had come to his aid in time.

. . . The battle was fought over the kingfisher's gift. Unknown to anyone, the trolls had switched the babies at birth. Now it was too late to exchange the children again, and only two things had the magic to right the mischief. One, a freshwater pearl, could enable the fairy babe to live underwater. The other, a slate-blue feather from the kingfisher's crest, would give the water sprite child the power of flight.

Just as the kingfisher was flying over the pond to the beach near the tree where the Tamarack family lived, the trolls attacked. Seven of them rose in a group out of the cattails, flinging rotten fish heads and entrails at the bird. The sight of them, eyes glittering behind the black muck and stinking vegetation that streamed from their hairy bodies, was enough to make anyone recoil. They must have lain in the shallow water, breathing through hollow rushes, until the right moment.

Stunned both by the sight and the vile missiles pelted at him, the kingfisher dropped the gifts into the inky depths of the pond. The pearl began to sink, but was found in time by the water sprites. The feather, meanwhile, drifted on the water's surface. Tamarack ran to the sand spit and launched his raft to go after it, but at that moment, before he or the bird could get to it, a great fish rose, took the feather in its mouth, and plunged back into the depths of the pond. It was the hornpout, one of the trolls' pets. Unless the feather could be retrieved, Meadowsweet would never fly!

Quickly, Tamarack baited his strongest fishhook and line with a worm from his bait basket and flung it into the water. There was a pause, and then the raft lurched as the greedy fish sucked in the bait. There was another, longer pause, while the pond seemed like a glass mirror suspended in midair. Then Tamarack heaved back on the line with his whole body, doubling it quickly around the end of one of the logs of his raft. As he did, the fish felt the hook bite into its jaw and the pond was shattered by his fury. Water began to swirl around Tamarack's ankles as the raft was dragged downward.

With a rattling cry of anger, the kingfisher swooped and caught the fishing line in his strong bill. Then, with powerful wings, the bird backpedaled in midair, dragging the fish up out of the depths to the edge of the beach. The hornpout's eyes bulged. Its skin was slimy and black, its belly pale and yellowish.

The raft bobbed in the shallows. Tamarack leapt off and splashed ashore. There, in a flurry of water, the monster thrashed, trying relentlessly to stab Tamarack with his trio of spikes, one supporting his dorsal fin and one hidden in the pectoral fin behind each set of gills. It was more than just a battle for the feather now—the hornpout was trying to kill him. Armed with only a carved rose-thorn knife, Tamarack fought grimly, dodging the deadly barbs, any of which could inflict a festering wound that might result in death. The kingfisher tried to drag the fish farther out of the water, but it was too heavy.

Once, for a moment, Tamarack seemed to have the beast trapped between two stones at the water's edge. "Agree to return the kingfisher's gift, and I will release you," Tamarack cried, pressing his knife into the soft flesh beneath the gills. Behind him the kingfisher beat his wings in fury. But the hornpout would have none of it. Snakelike, it surged at them, with nothing less than murder in its eyes. Tamarack twisted aside, managing to slash the creature's belly as he did. The water began to redden. Time and again, Tamarack closed with his knife only to be flung away by a powerful blow from the fish's tail. Once, his head struck a rock. He staggered to his feet, blinded by blood trickling into his eyes, dazed and exhausted. A hornpout is a fish that does *not die easily, and now the fish had him cornered in the water and would not let him gain the safety of the beach. Then there was a cry, like gravel tumbling over a cliff, and a flash of gray-blue as the kingfisher hurtled downward. Two, three, four blows from his lancelike bill and the hornpout quivered and finally lay still.*

The two friends stared at each other in exhaustion. The king-fisher's gift to Meadowsweet was lost—hidden somewhere under the water—but only one feather could be given, or the kingfisher must give his life as well—and they had barely escaped alive just now. . . .

IN HER MEMORY, FRANNY SNUGGLED INTO THE CURVE OF Papa's arm. The good, strong smell of Papa tickled her nostrils, not strong like a bad smell—strong like nothing could ever happen to her as long as Papa was there. Once she told Papa that when their maid, Ruth, let her try pressing the clothes, she could tell which were his things by their spicy, crisp scent as much as by the lack of ruffles. Papa was embarrassed.

"I hope I don't smell *that* much," he said with a laugh.

"No, Papa, it's not like that. It's nice, like the smell of apples or snow," she explained. Franny couldn't think what Mama smelled like, because Mama always wore perfume and never seemed to get close enough for Franny to really know.

Franny felt herself slip back to her other world. The next part of the story was the fight with the great orb weaver spider, who eagerly captured the flightless fairy child.

"No, vile net spinner," cried Tamarack, "you shall not claim this child of mine! Give the princess up!"

The huge web shook the marsh grasses as Mag's gorgeous yellow and black body, with its wicked, clutching legs, danced toward him. She clicked her jaws as she charged, and poisonous spittle bubbled at the corners of her mouth. Fury glittered red in her many eyes. Behind her, Meadowsweet cried and struggled with the masses of sticky thread that bound her.

Queen Iris screamed. Water sprite or not, this was the babe she had nursed from infancy and loved as her own. Her natural child would be raised a stranger, but happy, in the underwater realm. Meadowsweet might never fly, and her dark beauty and liquid eyes would perhaps seem strange, but she was her very own dear child. . . .

Then Franny remembered Mama's clear, certain voice breaking the story's spell. "Really, Arthur, it's time for Franny to go to sleep now."

"Oh, Mama, just one minute more! Papa's getting to the good part."

"And it can wait. Goodness knows these stories go on forever. Eight o'clock is bedtime." Franny's mother shook her head once briskly, so that the golden tendrils around her delicate features quivered. Franny sighed. What harm would it do if Papa told just a little more of the story? Crossly, she hitched herself down under the covers, trying to twist her nightdress straight. Mama's rules were rules.

Papa's lips brushed Franny's forehead and he said,

14

"There's always tomorrow, Sweet." Franny heard him sigh as he turned out the light and followed her mother out into the hall.

The next night she turned to Papa as he was about to begin her bedtime story, and she said, "I know what you work on at night when Mama and I are asleep!"

Papa's eyebrows went up. "You do?"

"Yes. Sometimes I get up and see the light on under your study door and hear your pen scratching. And I saw the stories in the drawer."

Papa chuckled and squeezed her shoulders playfully. "Franny, are you a snoop?"

Franny was suddenly worried. "Not a mean snoop, Papa. I was just curious about what was in there. It's the same stories you tell me when I say, 'Read me a story out of your own mouth.' " She wanted Papa to know that it had been like magic when she recognized the words, in his beautiful, curly handwriting—the same stories he had been telling her for as long as she could remember. She loved Papa's stories better than any of those in the red, violet, and yellow fairy books that Mama had given her and later taken away. . . .

———•———

THE BIG CAR LURCHED OVER A POTHOLE, AND FRANNY looked through the open car window at the stone wall, thick with poison ivy, that ran alongside the road. Papa had told her that the early settlers built it long ago, when this was new farmland, and Wayland just an isolated country village. Stone by stone, sometimes dragging a single boulder by itself on a sledge behind a team of oxen, they had built these miles of walls. It was in her history book in school too, the one she had barely looked at since last November.

Now many of the old stone walls ran through woods, where the pastures that the first farmers had worked so hard to clear had been let go and forgotten. Franny tried to concentrate on the wall, but it kept turning into a blur of gray and green.

Then at last, the car slowed. Franny opened her eyes and saw that they were passing between two square, stone gateposts, each higher than her head. Set into the one on her right was a plaque that read MORROW. It was weathered bluish green, like the statue of Washington in Boston Common. Moss grew on the mortar between the stones. The long, curving drive passed between two rows of white pines, like a shadowy hallway. Franny smelled the pitchy oldness of the trees. The car's tires, on pine needles and gravel, grumbled like waves on a pebble beach. At the end of the tunnel of pines stood the big, rectangular brick house, its shape partly hidden by a shaggy coat of English ivy. Several of the shades in the upstairs windows were drawn partway down, so that the house seemed to be looking out at the world through half-closed eyes.

Quickly Franny sat up, tried to smooth her hair, and

crammed her hat back onto her head with the backs of her hands. Then, again holding the basket very carefully, she waited for the car to come to a stop. As long as Papa was gone and she had to be at this place, Franny would take very good care of what was the most real thing she could think about now, Tamarack and his family.

Chapter Three

"I'LL TAKE THE BASKET AND YOUR HAT, MISS," A VOICE RASPED.

Franny looked up at Mrs. Stark, the housekeeper, who held the door open for her. She remembered Mrs. Stark. She had been there forever—since Papa was a boy. Not that she was exactly a beloved member of the family but, "She always kept the house in perfect order and I guess Mother was too lost in her own thoughts to understand what she was really like," Papa had told Franny. She was a large woman, not so very tall or fat, just big—with a bosom that was hard not to stare at. It was like the prow of a barge that fought and crashed against the sea, rather than riding gracefully through it.

Once Franny and Papa had rung the doorbell and hidden in the shrubbery just to see Mrs. Stark's face, with its jutting jaw and pale, colorless eyes, pucker into a mask of annoyance. Secretly, Papa called Mrs. Stark the Sea Hag. It was a good name, Franny thought, because up close, she could almost feel the woman's chilly bitterness, and her voice had a peculiar break in it that made Franny think of a seagull that had screamed itself hoarse.

She peered beyond Mrs. Stark into the dim hallway. A young woman who must be the new maid hung back, watching. There was no sign of Grandmother.

Franny let Mrs. Stark take her hat, but she stepped back from the hand that reached for her basket. For a moment it actually clutched at the handle. When Mrs. Stark realized that Franny was not going to let go, she inhaled sharply, eyed Franny as if she were adding up the price of a soup bone, and croaked, "Ida, you may go up and show Miss Morrow her room and help her unpack."

The maid called Ida stepped forward shyly. She reminded Franny of Mr. Van Reusen's new Morgan filly, Lark. Both were slim, dark, and neat, with long, graceful limbs. Lark would trot to the fence, her large eyes seeming to beg for a gentle hand on her neck, but at the same time, she trembled because the man who had owned her before had hit her.

Ida said, "Right this way, if you please, miss." Her words were softened and curled around the edges so that Franny thought they seemed like a different language. Franny, still holding the basket, followed Ida up the stairs. Henry came up behind them with her suitcase.

On the landing, Franny stopped a moment with her mouth open. The birds! How could she ever have forgotten the birds? There were dozens of them, stuffed and mounted in big glass bell jars on the wide shelf, preening, stretching, even seeming to flutter or sing—but all frozen, hushed. A scattering of sunlight angled through the window over the stairs and lighted them up like jewels.

Franny didn't know all the kinds. She saw scarlet, black, lemon yellow, rusty brown—birds posing on real twigs with nests, birds perched on clusters of dried flowers, birds upside down, pecking at bark. One tiny bird glowed such a pure blue that it seemed like a scrap of summer sky. Another wore a patch of gold at its throat and a velvety black mask over its eyes like a robber. Franny knew blue jays, robins, and chickadees from her yard in Cambridge, but these birds must be from somewhere very far away and exotic, a dusky jungle or a jade isle in a turquoise sea. She stared at them a long moment, in silence, hearing silence, trying to imagine the missing trickles and chatter of bird voices. Then she came to herself, realizing suddenly that Ida and Henry were both patiently waiting for her.

Henry set Franny's suitcase on the rack at the foot of the bed. Franny saw him gaze awkwardly at Ida for a moment. She was sure he wanted to say something to her, but Ida pretended not to see him and bent her head to unlatch the suitcase. Henry cleared his throat and touched his hat to Franny. "I hope you have a nice summer here, miss," he mumbled. Once again, Franny knew he was trying to be kind. She tried to smile a small, grateful smile at him before he went away.

Ida stepped over to the dresser and half opened a drawer

to demonstrate. "You'll be wantin' to put your things in here. I'll just be hangin' your dresses in the closet." Again, the words seemed to dance in the air in a way Franny had never heard before. Henry's rough New Hampshire accent, which sounded a little like a plow clanking through rocky ground, was somewhat familiar to her, but Ida's was different. Then she remembered. Nana had told her that Grandmother's new maid was "practically straight off the boat from Ireland." But the way Nana had said it hadn't prepared Franny for the musical sweet-sadness that was Ida.

"Now, that's a tidy bit of stitchery." Ida unfolded the half-finished sampler that Nana made Franny work on every Sunday afternoon. It read: "The things I love are pictured here, my friend, my posies, and my dolly-dear." It was to be a birthday present for Molly Greene, who lived across Mount Auburn Street and down two doors, and who had been Franny's best friend as long as she could remember. But Molly only wanted to play tea parties with her doll, Nanette, that her father had brought her from France. One day she said to Franny, "All you ever talk about, since your papa died, is your stupid, make-believe fairies. I'm sick of them!" The last time Franny played with her, Molly didn't even want to play dolls, she just giggled about a boy in their class, Tommy Swarting.

Franny scowled. Why did Nana have to send the sampler with her? It was such an old-fashioned thing to do. None of the other girls she knew had to make one—besides, she didn't feel that way about Molly or dolls anymore. But Nana said that all girls should learn to make fine stitches and that the only way to do it was to sew a sampler. Franny sighed. She hoped no one here would make her work on it.

Ida lifted a small cardboard box from the suitcase. Franny set her basket hurriedly on the bed and almost snatched the box from Ida's hands. She put it carefully in one of the top drawers without explaining. In it, with a few charred scraps of paper, was the Tamarack family's luggage.

"Take a moment to wash up then." Franny saw Ida's eyes flicker toward her bandaged hands, then look away. "Your grandmother'll be waitin' to see you, I'm sure. She's in the garden."

The door closed behind her, and Ida's steps clicked away down the long wooden floor of the upstairs hall. Franny didn't move for a few moments. The room seemed white and fluttery. Empty. This same room, which Grandmother now used as her guest room because it was at the top of the stairs, had been Papa's room when he was a boy.

Tamarack had been a boy then too. Franny knew all about how, unknown to his father, young Tamarack used to scramble up the side of the house, clinging to the tough little roots of the ivy, to this very room to visit Papa. She could see the ivy leaves fringing the windowsill.

Suddenly she was aware of a tiny, insistent thumping coming from under the lid of the basket. She lifted the lid. Meadowsweet tumbled out onto the bedspread with a cross little chatter that turned into squeaking giggles as she landed with a bounce. She held her lap robe, rolled into a bundle, tightly in her arms. A moment later Tamarack climbed nimbly over the basket's rim and dropped down beside his daughter. Iris didn't follow.

"I shall tear my dress if I climb basketry. Going up and down furniture is bad enough. I'm not a squirrel, you know!"

Ever so gently, Franny placed her left hand inside the basket next to Iris. "I'll help you out," she said.

"Oh, Franny, I'll hurt your poor fingers!"

"No you won't. You hardly weigh a thing."

So Iris seated herself carefully on Franny's palm, holding tightly to the bandage around her thumb, and nodded her head when she was ready. Her wings fluttered, in spite of herself, as she was lifted out. They shimmered palest emerald, with long tails and delicate golden veins, just for an instant. Then she tucked them carefully closed.

"Oh, Mama, I don't care if you fly," said Meadowsweet, rolling her eyes.

But Iris answered, "We must remember who we are, my dear. Flying simply is not dignified."

Queen Iris flicked imaginary dust from her cape and began to unfasten it. She took a few steps across the bed, looking around at Franny's new lodgings. Then she caught sight of the furry bundle Meadowsweet was unwrapping and cuddling in her arms. "Oh, no, Meadowsweet, you haven't brought that animal?" She looked at Tamarack but he only shrugged and grinned.

"No harm done, my love," he said. "A child's got to have a pet, I say. Stripesy might shed a bit, but at least 'Sweet didn't fetch along the newt. You always said yourself the furry pets were nicer than the cold, damp ones."

Meadowsweet's face glowed. She lifted Stripesy to her shoulder and snuggled her cheek into the glossy black and orange fur. "You'll see, Mama, Stripesy won't be any trouble at all, will you, girl?" The woolly bear caterpillar began to purr.

Queen Iris gave Tamarack another look and sniffed. "If we allow her to adopt every poor lost beast with a sore foot or a hungry stomach, we'll soon have a menagerie," she said.

"Mama, I couldn't leave her floating on that leaf in the middle of a thunderstorm. In another moment she would have been swept right into the brook!"

"Would you like to wash up?" Franny offered, trying to change the subject.

She tied the sash of her dressing gown carefully to one of the bedposts so that Tamarack and his family could use it for climbing up and down, and led the way to the bathroom. Iris glanced around fearfully before tucking up her skirts and letting herself gracefully down to the floor.

"It's all right, dearie," Tamarack assured her. "There aren't any cats. The Sea Hag was here in my day too, and believe me, she don't like them one bit. There's bound to be some in the barn, but you'll find the cats are a good sort in this neighborhood. Plenty of mice there, so they're well fed. The worst danger in the house is mousetraps. Mrs. Stark uses a lot of those. Meadowsweet, keep your eyes open and mind Stripesy stays clear of them!"

Meadowsweet nodded, but rolled her eyes again so that Franny guessed she was wishing she could just fly like any ordinary fairy child. All her parents' warnings and fretting could be so tiresome. "Papa, tell me again about the kingfisher's feather," Meadowsweet asked.

"Well, when it was discovered that the trolls had switched you babies (you in your floating water lily cradle, with the other babe in her nest of down), my friend the kingfisher was to give you each a gift. You see, we never knew that you had been changed in your cradle until it came time for your wings to grow and you to be starting to flutter and the other to be learning to dive. By then we loved you, and the water sprites loved her, and it was beyond changing things back. But your mother wept because you couldn't fly, and the water sprite mother wept because her babe couldn't breathe underwater, so the kingfisher tried to make it right. As the guardian of the pond, he felt responsible for letting such a thing happen. The trolls were no friends of his! But he had magic only for two gifts, no more—the pearl and the feather."

"And the feather was lost," sighed Meadowsweet, who really knew the story almost by heart.

"Yes, it was lost when the trolls flung fish heads at him. You know the rest, how the great hornpout swam up and sucked the feather into his maw and took it down into the depths of the pond before the kingfisher could recover and get it back."

"And then you lured that fish and hooked and fought him!"

"Yes, but we never found the feather, although the kingfisher dove time and again trying to find it. Perhaps it was the hornpout's mate that we killed on the beach that day, or perhaps he'd already carried the feather to his troll master to hide—and you know that trolls are *hiders*. They take more pleasure out of hiding something that someone wants, like socks, or hairpins, or left-hand gloves, than in using it themselves. The more a person wants a thing, the better they like to hide it. They wouldn't think of destroying it and missing the fun of watching you hunt for it."

"And the kingfisher could not give another feather, or he would lose his own power of flight and perish." Meadowsweet sighed with satisfaction. Even though she desperately longed to feel the breeze under her slim body, and see the world from the air, she loved the story of the lost feather. "What happened to the kingfisher, Papa?"

Her father looked at her sadly. "We may never know, 'Sweet. He was wounded in the fight, and might have died, but your mother cured him with a salve. Some time later, he disappeared. I found marks of another struggle on the beach, but no clue to explain what happened. Now we hunt for the feather whenever we come back, but that's not very often. You know the way of things—once our folk adopt a person, we stay as long as we are needed. Franny needed us with her in Cambridge. But now that she's come here, we can have another look, though really, the chances of finding it are slim."

They had reached the bathroom by then, and Franny helped them up onto the sink. In the soap dish was a new package of soap. The wrapper read: "White, Pure, Floating, Fairy Soap." Franny smiled. It was her favorite kind—did someone know? "Have you a little fairy in your home?" asked the message under the picture. The fairy child was plump and curly haired, seated on the oval bar of soap. She didn't look much like Meadowsweet, but Franny nodded to herself. "Yes, there is a fairy in this house—more than one!" she whispered.

Meadowsweet, still holding her caterpillar, seated herself on the rubber sink stopper hanging from its chain, and began swinging back and forth. They giggled over the secret as Franny unwrapped the soap carefully without tearing the paper.

Gingerly, trying not to get her bandages wet, Franny dampened the washcloth, soaped it, and washed her face. She couldn't very well wash her hands. Her teeth clenched as she tried to rinse and wring out the washcloth with her fingertips. Tamarack, Iris, and Meadowsweet rubbed their hands against the wet bar of soap, and rinsed in droplets of water that Franny trickled on the edge of the sink for them. Stripesy crawled over to a clean droplet and lapped at it thirstily.

Iris liked warm water, but Meadowsweet and Tamarack liked theirs better cold. "Ugh, how can you bear it like that?"

asked Iris as she watched Tamarack douse his face. Her husband only grinned and shook a tiny, icy spray at her from the wet ends of his hair.

"Cold water feels rejoicing, Mama," explained Meadowsweet seriously, her eyes sparkling like raindrops. Then she turned to Tamarack. "Papa, where are we going to live while we're here?"

Tamarack was drying his face on a corner of Franny's towel. "I thought perhaps we'd fix up the old mansion under the roots of the larch tree by the pond. It's where you were born and I grew up, you know."

"Oh, no, Tamarack," cried Iris, "not by the pond—she'd be down under that dark water all the time, with Lord knows what swimming about. I won't have it. It's much too dangerous."

"Please, Mama, I've never swum in a pond before," begged Meadowsweet.

Iris started to sniffle. "I couldn't bear the worry. We couldn't help you if anything happened."

"But Mama, I'm a water sprite. I'd be all right."

"Please, Tamarack," Iris pleaded with her husband, "not the Larch Tree Mansion. Isn't there someplace else?"

Tamarack patted her arm. "Never you mind, it just so happens there is, and I think you'll both like it very much."

Without really meaning to, Franny looked into the mirror and saw her own face. Its roundness and freckles always surprised her. Meadowsweet wasn't like that at all. Meadowsweet was dark and slender. But Papa always said that Franny had fairy eyes. . . .

It made her think of when she was five and Mrs. Koslowski was fitting her for a Christmas dress. Nana had pursed her lips and frowned. "Better not use so much lace, Polly, it only points up her plainness." So she was plain.

That night when Franny had cried over it, Papa held her up to the mirror. "True fairies have green eyes like you, Sweet, and they always grow into great beauties." Franny had studied her reflection. Her eyes didn't look very green. They were an uncertain color that made her think of grass in November. Maybe that was what people called hazel. But Papa took his smoking jacket from its hook, wrapped her in its emerald satin folds, and held her up to the mirror again. "See?" And her eyes *were* green. . . .

Franny saw Iris standing on tiptoe beside her, trying to peek into the mirror herself. She couldn't quite see, and when Meadowsweet was busy paddling her bare feet in the puddles of water on the sink's rim, Franny saw Iris flutter her wings, to lift herself up a moment, so that she could fuss a stray tendril of hair back into place.

The sight and feel of water made Meadowsweet's cheeks flush. "Franny, fill up the tub so I can take a swim," she begged, tugging at Franny's pinky, but Franny shook her head.

"I have to go see my grandmother now. We can do that later."

Chapter Four ⁓

TO SAVE TIME, FRANNY GAVE THEM A RIDE BACK TO THE bed in the bunched-up front of her skirt. She thought she ought to do something else to make herself presentable to Grandmother, but then she noticed that the bedroom window was open. Franny stepped over to it. She did not see the formal garden below, the barn, vegetable patch, or gardener's cottage. She ignored the view of orchard, woods, pasture, and just down the road a little way, the shining oval that was Larch Pond. She was looking into the thick ivy that grew up and around the window ledge. Tamarack and his family could easily climb up and down through the ivy, unseen by hawks or weasels. They would, of course, feel smothered in a human house. This way they could set up a summer home nearby, perhaps in the garden below, and travel safely up and down for visits. It was just like Papa had told her. It was perfect. . . .

"Miss Morrow!"

Franny whirled around. She was still kneeling by the window. The basket lay open on the bed. Quickly Franny scrambled over to it, snatched it up, and replaced the cover.

"Little ladies do not keep their grandmothers waiting."

It was Mrs. Stark. With a heavy tread, she stalked over to the armchair beside the bed and twitched the tatted lace antimacassars on the arms.

I haven't even been here long enough to muss them up, thought Franny with a surge of resentment.

The woman wore a black uniform with a white collar. The skin of her hands, throat, and face was ash colored, her tightly curling hair steel gray. Franny couldn't look at her eyes, because they were dull, almost lifeless, and it made her shiver. They were focused on Franny now, and, skin crawling, she felt the woman's gaze inspecting her from head to foot.

She already knew how straight and dirt brown her hair was, but Mrs. Stark somehow made it feel straighter and browner. She licked the corners of her mouth. (Was there a crumb from breakfast that she'd missed?) The eyes lingered on her hands, with their damp bandages, holding the little wicker basket. She felt them roam over her white sailor dress with its pleated skirt. Franny stood up straighter. Mama was always particular about her clothes. Franny knew they were clean and neatly pressed, even if her hem had been let out so that she could wear the skirt another year. The eyes seemed to examine each round little button of her shoes. . . . (Had she scuffed the toes already? Were they dusty from the automobile ride?)

When the gaze was finished, Franny felt as if the woman knew everything about her, had rifled through every secret drawer in her heart—but it was all twisted and wrong somehow.

Hugging her basket protectively, Franny followed Mrs. Stark down the stairs. It was such a dark house! The wainscoting and beams were dark brown. Heavy drapes, the color of a pine forest, hung at the windows. At the foot of the stairs hung a brass candleholder embossed with a picture of a lamplighter, but it was tarnished nearly black and there was no candle. Franny looked into the parlor as they passed. She saw a stuffed sofa and chairs with more tatted lace covers on the arms and backs, each neatly in place. There was a grand piano with massive black legs, and a great brown bearskin rug on the floor. On each side of the fireplace were the paintings that Grandmother Morrow had brought with her from Tennessee.

Franny stopped and looked curiously now at the paintings. General Lee sat on his good horse, Traveller, in front of a plantation house. Franny thought he looked tired and sad. Even Traveller had a weary look in his big soft eyes. It reminded Franny of the eyes of the skinny old horse that pulled the ragman's cart up Mount Auburn Street on Saturday mornings, except that Traveller didn't hang his head, but held it proudly. Sad eyes, proud head.

The other painting showed woods and mountains. Up close were shaggy trees that melted into a forever-ness of humped and rolling blue mountains rising through a mist that was, Franny thought, very rightly called smoky. She found suddenly that she was not breathing. The paintings had somehow caught and held her. Mrs. Stark cleared her throat impatiently.

Franny tried to swallow the rising feeling of dread and followed the housekeeper out a door and through an arched brick entryway hung with ivy. They went down three wide stone steps to a circular terrace, in the center of which stood a sundial. Franny read words on it: "I count none but sunny hours." In between all the stones crept a mossy little plant with tiny lavender flowers. It smelled sweet in the early June sun.

The terrace was closed in by fieldstone walls. Steps led down to the lawn from each side of a bed of lilies of the valley. There was a gnarled and leaning crab apple tree, its pink petals scattered on the stones. Several old white birch trees stood in the broad lawn, their trunks nearly as big around as cheese boxes. Suddenly Franny remembered. She and Papa were rolling down that sloping lawn and she was seeing the big birch trees whirling by. Then there was something about grass stains and Mama scolding. She couldn't remember exactly.

Through a wrought iron arch at the far end of the garden to her left, Franny saw the strangest little tree. It looked like an enchanted tree out of some old tale. Its trunk and branches twisted and knotted themselves almost as if it were alive and moving with muscles under the scaly bark. It grew upward, then outward, then downward in cascades of long, drooping branches whose leaves brushed the ground. Franny longed to slip into the shady hiding place under that tree.

In the walled rose garden to the right, they found her grandmother, busy with a small pair of clippers. Mrs. Stark abandoned Franny then, without saying a word. Grandmother didn't turn around. Franny waited, shifting uneasily from one foot to the other, her hands, and the basket, held tightly behind her back.

She stole a look at her grandmother. She was a tiny woman, but even tending her roses, she seemed to hold herself straighter than anyone Franny had ever seen—as straight as one of the columns on the front of the old plantation house in the painting, Franny thought. The braids wound around her head were nearly white. Untidy wisps had come loose from the hairpins here and there. Her dress was worn and faded. The sleeves were rolled up at the elbows. People didn't wear such full skirts now. Grandmother would look old-fashioned and out of place in Cambridge.

Franny had almost decided to go back to her room when Grandmother finally turned around. The old woman tilted her head to the side and smiled a little stiffly. Franny's mind turned to the portrait of the young girl with the dreaming eyes and flyaway hair that hung in Papa's study . . . *the belle of Knoxville.* She could see that Grandmother Morrow had indeed once been that girl, but something more than years had changed the expression in her eyes. Then Franny was suddenly reminded of one of the birds in the jars. Grandmother was alive, yet in some way she seemed frozen in time. It felt as though a wall, invisible, yet hard like glass, stood between Grandmother and herself.

"You've come then, Franny." There was a hint of the South in her voice. "And your hands are better, I hope?"

Behind her back, Franny's hands clenched into fists holding the handle of the basket. "Yes, Grandmother."

"I hope your ride out was satisfactory. Henry is a good driver."

Franny's eyes moved to the rosebushes surrounding her grandmother. They were covered with buds, a few beginning to unfold, pink, pure white, deep crimson, pale orange. Her mouth started to open. Without thinking, she turned, taking it all in. She reached out a hand to touch a cream-colored bud. The faintest hint of peach color edged its half-opened petals.

"That one is called Memory. It won first prize at the garden show in Boston." Franny noticed that Grandmother's hand strayed to a little gold heart at her throat as she spoke, in a gesture that looked like an old habit.

Meadowsweet and Iris would be enchanted, thought Franny. They would make Tamarack climb up by the thorns and hack off blooms for them with his sword. They would lift the sweet-smelling petals to their cheeks and stroke them. They would be like Mama at the seamstress's shop, surrounded by all the lovely fabrics—damasks, chiffons, and silks—folding, tucking, planning new dresses, humming to themselves. Maybe they could see the roses through the little spaces in the wicker of the basket right now. She very nearly leaned down to ask them if they could.

"Do you like my roses?"

"Yes," she answered simply.

"Would you like some to put in your basket?"

"Nooo," stammered Franny in confusion. "I already have my . . . my dolls in it."

Grandmother Morrow nodded. Then she said, in her cool, polite voice that made Franny feel like a complete stranger, "I'm afraid you'll be bored here, Franny. I'm a dull old woman. I like my books, my birds, and my flowers. I go on walks, and to Saturday morning lectures, but that's about all. You're welcome to accompany me. You may play about the house, garden, and barn as you wish. I'm sorry your father's and uncles' ponies are long since gone. I still keep a milk cow, Marigold, and our old carriage horse, Bobby Burns. He's nearly twenty-five. When your grandfather bought the Cadillac, he wanted to sell Bobby, but I wouldn't let him—the pasture would look so empty without a horse. . . . He's quite gentle, but he's not a riding horse. I never did learn to drive an automobile, but I was a good hand at driving Bobby."

Franny was looking curiously at Grandmother Morrow's eyes. They weren't brown or blue. Suddenly she recognized the same uncertain green of her own eyes. For a few seconds the invisible glass between them seemed gone.

Then Grandmother Morrow said, "You must miss your father, Franny. I know I do. Sometimes it seems too much to bear, losing both your grandfather and Arthur. It is very hard for a child to have a parent die—or the other way around. . . ."

Instantly the barrier was up. Franny wouldn't hear it. Papa was not . . . Grandmother should not have said that word, she thought furiously. She blinked hard, trying to stop the blinding rush of tears, turned abruptly, and fled back to her room.

Chapter Five ≈

It took a stern lecture from Iris to get Franny to go down to supper. "People say the most ridiculous things, Franny. Your grandmother was probably talking about someone else. Mrs. Matilda Nettlebody once came screeching to tell me that my house in the sweet viburnum bush was on fire, which was entirely untrue. It was Whiskersnoop's hunting camp that was ablaze. It was a total loss, and it was no one's fault but his own for building it too close to your father's incinerator." Together Iris and Meadowsweet were pulling a comb through Franny's hair as she lay on the bed sniffling. Tamarack couldn't deal with tears. He was busy clearing out the old trail down through the ivy.

"Anyway," Iris continued, "you are your papa's fairy princess and as such, must be strong, forgiving, and wise in the social graces. You must grit your teeth and attend meals, even if the company is not to your liking."

"Besides," added Meadowsweet with a practical shake of

her finger (Meadowsweet could be bossy when she was hungry), "you'll starve, and so shall we."

So a few minutes later, basket in hand, Franny crept down the stairs past the jewel-like birds, stepped cautiously into the dining room, and slipped into a chair across from Grandmother. Franny looked around. Grandmother's wallpaper didn't look like wallpaper at all. It was a painted picture of moss-green countryside with horses and hounds galloping through it, only here and there you could see a seam and the picture repeated itself. There was a heavy sideboard built of honey-colored wood, trimmed with a zigzag design made out of darker wood. The big, deep drawers on each side were built in curves, like fat bellies. On top of it, a silver tea service glimmered before a large gilt-framed mirror.

It didn't look like a family's room, but Franny's papa and her two uncles had sat at this big table every night. Everything was so fancy, it was hard to imagine. Papa was the youngest, Franny knew, and he had often told her how he usually had something in his pocket, like a bottle of ink, or rubber bands, that got him in trouble. Uncle Edward was serious and scientific. Uncle George was a joker then, just like he was now. Franny wondered if the three boys had fought and all talked at once, like the Van Reusen boys did the times she had dinner at their house. Had Papa and his brothers come to the table with dirty hands, knocked over glasses of milk, and had to be told not to rock back on the chair legs? She could almost hear the echoes of that long ago life, but now this room was very quiet.

Grandmother nodded to Franny and spoke to her as she sat down, saying, "It's a lovely evening, don't you think? The june bugs will be out tonight. I could almost believe I was back in Tennessee when it's warm like this."

Franny said nothing.

"Mr. B has sent up some nice lettuce and early radishes from the garden, you must try some."

Franny still said nothing. Grandmother grew quiet. Carefully, Franny slipped the cover off the basket in her lap so that she could share her dinner.

Ida served them boiled potatoes, peas, and sliced beef. "Mrs. Stark is a good enough cook, though somewhat plain," said Grandmother with a little laugh. "I don't believe she likes to try out new recipes, but she does run this house like a Swiss clock."

Franny rolled peas about with her fork. After a bit, she glanced up at the silver candelabra in the center of the table. She saw that Meadowsweet was creeping along one of its twisting branches, still barefoot, holding her arms out to balance herself: Stripesy had crawled all the way out to the end and was stuck halfway up one of the candlesticks. Now the caterpillar wanted to come down, but she was afraid. She arched her orange and black body and danced back and forth on two of her front feet, whimpering in fear. Queen Iris plunked herself down on the rim of the saltcellar and wrung her hands. As Franny watched, Meadowsweet teetered for a moment, then reached her wayward pet and coaxed her down into her arms.

Out of the corner of her eye, Franny saw Tamarack over by Grandmother's terrarium. It stood on a carved wooden chest beside the French doors leading to the screened porch. He gave a little nod when he saw that Meadowsweet had caught Stripesy. Franny thought maybe Tamarack trusted his daughter more than Iris did. Now he slid back the glass cover of the terrarium and nimbly let himself down over the edge to drop in among the glossy green partridgeberry vines. He plucked one of the bright red fruits and bit into it like an apple. Then he pressed his nose against the terrarium glass, schoolboy-fashion, and grinned at Franny, still chewing. She giggled.

Mrs. Stark, bringing in the rolls, raised an eyebrow and glared at Franny. Franny ignored her. Grandmother continued to eat. Meadowsweet shinnied down to the tablecloth now and landed with a tiny thump. "See, Mama? I didn't fall," she said to Iris.

Franny propped the tip of the blade of her knife against her fork and draped her napkin over them. "Look, this is how you can make a tent," she whispered. "I could get you a napkin from the sideboard later if you want to go camping." She didn't see Mrs. Stark moving a step closer. Suddenly the tent toppled over, and as Franny reached quickly to grab it, her elbow bumped the gravy boat, slopping the rich brown stuff onto the clean linen. There was a hiss from Mrs. Stark's lips.

She called for Ida, who wiped the spill and slipped a towel under the tablecloth to protect the beautiful mahogany finish.

As Mrs. Stark placed the refilled gravy boat on the table, her voice sighed into Franny's ear like wind off a frozen sea, "Little ladies pay attention at table and keep their left hands quietly in their laps." Afterward when Franny put her hand to her ear, it actually felt cold. She looked up at Grandmother. But Grandmother, holding her knife and fork as if she were dining with a room full of guests, looked at her plate and continued eating her dinner. She hadn't seemed to notice the incident at all. Franny didn't know if she was being kind or if her mind was simply elsewhere. Grandmother's face gave no clue.

Later, as Franny was going upstairs, she overheard Mrs. Stark talking to Grandmother. "It isn't natural for a child to mumble and whisper to herself. It's almost as if she's seeing things that aren't there, as if she's touched in the head. It gives me tremors."

"Mrs. Stark, I'll thank you to remember that it's my grandchild you're talking about," Grandmother replied coolly. "She has suffered a great loss and her mother is ill. And I think it quite natural for children to talk to themselves and see things we do not."

For a moment, Franny felt something like gratitude for Grandmother's words, but then she remembered the horrible thing she had said about Papa.

Meadowsweet would be looking forward to their bath now. That was what she would do—she would go up and run the water, not too hot for Meadowsweet, and not too cool for herself. They would play the old game. She would float the bar of Fairy soap and giggle, watching her tiny friend scramble aboard the slick raft, lose her grip, rock, tip, and slip back into the water with a shriek and a splash. Maybe she would pull the loose snap from her petticoat and toss it for Meadowsweet to dive down and find. Meadowsweet loved diving. She could stay down as long as she wanted. Sometimes Franny would forget that she was under the water until she felt a tiny pinch on her backside that made her sit up with a startled little squeak.

Later, Franny climbed into bed and stared at the ceiling, waiting for sleep. She felt like she was in the middle of a white ocean, floating by herself in whiteness. Her thoughts began to move the same way they always did, in a slow, steady, circular march, always ending and starting again at the same place: Papa . . . if only Papa . . .

She remembered when Papa was just beginning to be sick. At first it seemed like an ordinary cold with sneezes and a cough. There must have been a lot happening at his office just then, because every night he was late coming home. One evening he missed the last car out from Boston and had to walk home three miles in driving sleet. In the morning he had a fever.

"Maybe it would be better to stay in bed and rest," said Mama, putting her hand on his forehead.

Papa smiled and brushed her away. Franny noticed that his

cheeks were flushed and his eyes very bright. "A little fever isn't going to keep me home, Elizabeth. I can rest once this contract is settled."

Mama fussed a little more and let him go. But when he stayed up late at night writing, in spite of his fever, she grew cross. Mama had never thought much of Papa's story writing, and now she seemed to blame that for his illness.

Two days later he came to breakfast wearing the same clothes he had been wearing the night before. His brown hair was rumpled, as if he'd been running his fingers through it, and he seemed, in a way, to be somewhere else. At first Mama was brisk, almost cold, like a March wind. Then suddenly, she stood up from the table and threw down her napkin, saying, "Honestly, Arthur, this is getting to be more than I can bear. You're no better and you refuse to get any rest. You've no right to be staying up all night when you're sick, writing those foolish stories. If you'd take care of yourself, you'd get better and you'd be able to keep up with your duties at the office. Sometimes I think your brothers keep you on out of charity, because you have a family—your heart just isn't in it. And what can my parents think? Here we are, just getting by, when you could be getting commissions every week, like George and Edward. You might just as well be teaching school after all." Then she bit her lip and began to cry.

Franny looked anxiously at Papa. She knew he had wanted to be a teacher once, but there had been the family business to carry on. Papa started to answer, but his words turned into a fit of coughing. Franny saw that there were blue circles under his eyes and a deep crease that appeared between his brows as he gasped for air. "I'm sorry, Elizabeth," he said quietly when he could talk again. "There's an editor in New York who says he'll look at the stories if I can get them ready by the tenth. I'll try to do better." His voice sounded like it hurt to speak.

Franny had suddenly been angry. "You've never read Papa's stories!" she shouted at Mama. "They're the best stories in the world! They're more real than anything. Don't you ever call them foolish!"

Mama stared at Franny and Franny stared back. It was strange. Mama looked, for a moment, like willful Titania from *A Midsummer Night's Dream*, tears still wet on her cheeks, and the loose curls around her face trembling. Suddenly Franny thought, Papa married Mama because she looks so much like a fairy. But she's not like a fairy, Franny told herself fiercely. She can't see things, like galloping cloud horses, moonbeam angels, oak leaves that turn into toads, or fairies. . . .

Then, as if she could hear Franny's thoughts, Mama said, in a voice like tight knots, "Franny, there are *no* such things as fairies."

Even when Papa did stay home from work a few days to rest, Mama still insisted that it was the late nights in his study that had made him so sick. And then one morning he couldn't get out of bed and Mama, her hands shaking, picked up the telephone receiver, turned the crank, and called for the doctor. . . .

———•———

FRANNY OPENED HER EYES AND STARED AGAIN AT THE ceiling. There was a rustling at the window ledge. She turned her head to see Tamarack, Iris, and Meadowsweet climbing out of the ivy. "It's a good garden, Franny," said Meadowsweet as they scrambled up onto the bed beside her. "There are lots of kinds of flowers, and there's the fattest toad you ever saw under the lupines."

Iris said, "We'll just sleep right in the basket tonight on your bedside table, and keep you company." Franny looked at her gratefully. She knew that tomorrow they would set up their home somewhere outdoors. They would feel stuffy and trapped, sleeping in a human's house, but just for tonight it would be good to have them beside her.

Tamarack came over and gave Franny a kiss on the tip of her nose. It felt like a snowflake, only not cold. "Best get some sleep, youngster, we've got lots to do tomorrow."

Chapter Six ⟿

"Young lady, I advise you to cooperate. I've known people to die of infection from burns less severe than yours. And you will *let go* of that basket."

It was the next morning and Mrs. Stark was trying to follow the doctor's orders to change the dressings on Franny's hands. The housekeeper wrestled the basket away, peered into it, snorted, "Why, it's as empty as a schoolgirl's head!" and smacked it down on the dresser. As she let go of the basket, she gave a little yelp. "Ouch!" She looked curiously at one of her fingers and shook it as if she had pricked it on something sharp. Franny clenched her hands behind her back and stared at the floor.

What had happened to her hands hurt inside her chest almost more than the blisters hurt her fingers. She had not cried when it happened. She had not cried, nor even looked, when Doctor Maddox treated them. She could make her face not show it, but on the inside the burning wouldn't stop. Nobody, not Mama, not Nana and Baba, or Grandmother Morrow,

47

and especially not Mrs. Stark, would ever know how much she hurt. She would rather take off all her clothes right here in front of her than show her hands to Mrs. Stark. The house-keeper sputtered and fumed, but Franny stared at the dark green, twisted vines and pinecone shapes in the carpet, re-membering. . . .

———•———

"FRANNY, THERE'S NO SUCH THING AS FAIRIES. YOU MUST stop believing that there are." Mama's voice was flat, as if she were almost too tired to speak. Franny half turned her head and saw her mother put out a hand, wanting to stroke her hair, but Franny turned back, staring away. She was in the backyard, clutching a handful of acorn tops. On the ground in front of her were pieces of moss, fungi, bark, little woven mats of grass, lean-tos built of twigs, intricately arranged. To most people it would look like a lovely child's play, but to Franny it was more. It had become something she couldn't *not* do. She had been at it since breakfast today, all day yesterday, and countless hours in the months before that.

Queen Iris had been in her bower, stitching the waistband of a new rhododendron blossom skirt. King Tamarack was in Meadowsweet's little twig chamber telling her a bedtime story. It was very late, but Iris was so busy with her sewing that she had forgotten about the time. Meadowsweet's bed was all made of lilac blooms. Franny thought it must be like snuggling into a purple heaven. "Papa will love it," she thought to herself. . . .

People said he was dead, but she wouldn't let it be true. Mama even said it was the stories that had killed him. But she was wrong. Mama thought the stories were bad, but they weren't. They were the best . . . they *were* Papa. That was why she couldn't let them stop.

There were the school reports that Franny hadn't bothered to look at. Notes from teachers saying that Franny talked to herself. If she could have seen herself at the dinner table, she would have seen an ordinary, nicely dressed child of twelve, eyes far away, lips moving, sometimes even gesturing with her hands, having to be reminded to eat. . . .

"Franny, you've got to stop this. Your papa's dead and fairies are not real."

She wouldn't hear. She wouldn't.

Then Mama noticed the mushrooms. Franny had dug them up carefully with a kitchen spoon. She had replanted them in a circle to make a fairy ring for Tamarack and his beautiful Queen Iris. They could hold Meadowsweet's birthday party here and all the shy little folk from the garden would come to dance when fireflies flashed and moonlight made the shadows blue. She had found some of the mushrooms under the spruce trees in the neighbor's backyard, some in the cemetery across the street, some right here in the grass. They were lovely: pink with white gills underneath, orange speckled, lavender, some stubby, some delicate. She hadn't hurt them a bit.

Then Mama seemed to go crazy. Her eyes were fixed on a pair of ghostly white mushrooms with lacy ruffles around their stems. "Franny, don't you know those are deadly poisonous!" Her face seemed turned into a mask of terror and rage. As Franny watched, frozen, she struck out with the toe of her shoe and smashed the fairy ring to pulp. She crushed the tiny bark huts, the table of twigs set with acorn-top dishes, crushed them and kicked the broken pieces into the grass.

Mama dragged Franny into the kitchen and scrubbed at her hands with hot water and soap, as if she would scrub the skin right off. She left Franny and ran, sobbing, upstairs. Franny heard her keep on going, up the stairs to the attic. Then she heard Mama's footsteps, stumbling, coming down, going into her bedroom.

For long moments, Franny stood alone in the kitchen. A strange odor began to seep into the air around her. What was it? Then she knew. Smoke. Burning paper. Suddenly she understood what Mama was doing. She rushed to the landing, screaming, "No, Mama!" Her feet on the stairs felt heavy and slow. The distance along the upstairs hall to Mama's door seemed forever. For a moment, the doorknob wouldn't turn. She couldn't open it! "Mama, no!" Then she gripped it harder and the door opened. She stood gasping in her mother's bedroom, not believing her mother could do such a thing, but it was too late.

She saw the empty box, the last sheets of paper burning. The curling flames in Mama's pretty bedroom fireplace with the gleaming brass andirons and the blue Delft tiles all around it. Large blackened leaves of ash floated, like strange birds, up the chimney. Franny tried to pull the pages out, to save something, anything, slapping at the fire, not feeling the burning.

Mama was crumpled on the floor, moaning half sentences. "Let her go . . . don't take her with you . . . I won't let you. . . ."

Coldly, Franny walked past her mother, back downstairs, and out to the garden, a few fragments of half-consumed manuscript clutched in her blackened hands. It was the maid, Ruth, who called Doctor Maddox and Nana DiCrista. . . .

———•———

IDA BROKE THE STANDOFF BETWEEN FRANNY AND MRS. Stark. She had been waiting to help, with strips of linen and the tin of lard. "Would ye let me do it, Franny? I'm a good hand with bandages. Then ye can have the basket back," she ventured timidly. Franny slowly raised her eyes to meet Ida's. She saw eyes that knew what pain was, not just pain of the body, but pain of the heart, and knew that like Grandmother Morrow and Henry, something in life had hurt Ida almost beyond bearing. And there was more. Franny found a deep, abiding kindness there. She nodded.

Mrs. Stark slapped the scissors into Ida's hand in exasperation. "That suits me," she croaked. "I've certainly got better things to do than to butt heads with a willful, troubled child."

She turned and steamed like a battleship back down to her kitchen.

Ida led Franny over to the chair, set the things on the bedside table, and motioned for Franny to sit down. Then she knelt and took Franny's hands in her own. "Let's see the poor little mitts," she said softly.

With utmost delicacy, the young woman snipped through the bandages and peeled them away. Franny bit her lip and looked over Ida's shoulder, studying the framed photograph that hung on the wall. It was of Papa and his brothers in a cart pulled by a fat pony with a stand-up mane. Ida rubbed the lard into the linen strips and rebandaged Franny's hands. "There now, 'tis not so bad as Mrs. Stark makes out. They're healing nicely. In another few days ye won't be needin' any dressings at all."

When it was finished, Franny looked after Ida gratefully. Surely she must have wondered, but she hadn't asked how Franny had burned her hands.

Chapter Seven ⌣

Now that she was dressed and her hands tended to, Franny supposed that she should go downstairs and eat breakfast. Looking to make sure that Ida was gone and Mrs. Stark was truly out of the way, she opened the lid of the basket and peered inside, asking anxiously, "Are you all right?"

"All right? That was the meanest witch I ever heard!" sputtered Meadowsweet, hands on hips and stamping a tiny foot. "She sounds like an old crow when she talks. Mama and I banged our heads together and we could have got concussion." Her eyes sparked with fury. Then, like sharp ice crystals suddenly melting to shining liquid, her mood changed and she sat down hard, laughing. "But did you see me stick Mama's hat pin in her finger?" she gasped.

Iris looked a little pale, but Tamarack patted her shoulder reassuringly. "We're fine, Franny," he said, "but that is surely one to watch out for!"

Taking the basket with her, Franny ventured downstairs.

On the landing she stopped suddenly. There was Grand-mother standing by the open door to the coat closet. She must have been out walking in the cool morning, for she had on a man's faded green sweater with holes in the elbows. A bunch of Indian paintbrushes and daisies lay on the hall table behind her, and there was a fresh smell, as if some of the breath of the morning meadow had followed her inside. Grandmother had taken Franny's little straw traveling hat down from the shelf where Mrs. Stark had put it when she arrived. There was a look of wonder on her face. Franny watched as, with uncertain fingers, the old woman touched the rosette of dark blue satin attached to the hatband and smoothed the two ribbons that trailed down over the brim.

When she saw Franny, she stiffened and quickly put the hat back on the closet shelf. "Good morning," she said.

"Good morning," Franny replied. Grandmother hung her sweater on a hook on the back of the closet door and led the way to the dining room. Franny thought maybe somehow it would be easier for them to talk now, but breakfast was as silent as dinner had been. Once or twice, Franny saw Grandmother glance at her, and saw something flicker across her face almost like cloud shadows chasing sunlight over a field. Franny couldn't think of anything to say and, it seemed, neither could Grandmother.

"I'm sorry to be so dull, Franny," she said finally when the meal was over. "My mind just seems to be elsewhere. I've a new bird book just come in by post from Boston, and I'm eager to have a look at it. I know I ought to think of something fun for you to do. Do you mind very much entertaining yourself?" She bit her lip and looked uncertainly at Franny.

Franny gripped the handle of her basket tightly. "I'm all right, Grandmother," she answered.

The old woman turned and went into her study, closing the door behind her. As Franny walked past the hall table, she saw the bunch of wildflowers lying on it, wilted and forgotten.

She pushed open the door that led out to the garden, stepped cautiously outside, and walked through the archway toward the strange little tree. Franny glanced over her shoulder at the house and thought she saw Grandmother, seated at the table in her study, look up and watch her through the window a moment, then go back to her work. Then Franny was on her knees, holding back the tips of the sweeping branches and peering into the dappled secret place behind them. She set down the basket and opened it. Tamarack climbed out, followed by the others. He tilted his head back, looking up into the branches, and smiled broadly, as if meeting an old friend. Then he strode over to the tree and patted the trunk affectionately. "You haven't changed a bit, old girl," he murmured. He turned to the others, drew his sword, and struck the tree ceremoniously with it. "We shall build a castle here, in the air," he announced.

Franny slipped off her shoes and stockings, and with a little bit of scrambling, her bound-up hands awkward and sore, she pulled herself up into the tree. At about the height of her head, there was a broad flat place where the limbs spread outward from the main trunk. The branches felt like strong arms. They were hard and cool, and the bark was rough, but they were part of a living thing and they held her safely. It was almost as if the tree cared about her. Franny sat there, with her skirt bunched up over her knees and the leaf shadows making a shifting pattern on her bare legs. She breathed in the smells of new leaves, old bark, and damp earth. The leaves were a whispering, green curtain between herself and the rest of the world.

In another moment Tamarack, Iris, and Meadowsweet appeared beside her. Iris brushed bits of bark from her moss-colored morning dress. "Oh, you three will make a squirrel out of me yet," she scolded, but her cheeks were pink with excitement. She gazed around at the sturdy branches that twisted in a maze under the canopy of leaves. Meadowsweet was already scampering about with Stripesy panting slowly after her as best she could.

Iris turned to Tamarack. "It's wonderful," she breathed. But then she grew practical. "Of course we shall need a ladder. It will never do to be always scrambling up and down."

Tamarack nodded. "Right-o, my love." He squinted along the branches where Franny's feet were resting. "Hmm. Very nearly level, I should think. It'll be a bit of work, but I think we can build a jolly tree house." He looked up at Franny. "What do you think, youngster?"

Franny grinned.

⸺•⸺

THEY SET TO WORK RIGHT AWAY. SHYLY, FRANNY APproached Ida in the kitchen. "Have you got any string and a pair of scissors?"

Ida was polishing silverware. She put down her tarnishy rag and wiped her hands on her apron. "Now, surely I do," she said, opening the drawer of the kitchen table and handing her a ball of twine and some shears. "Is it a project you're undertakin'?"

"Well, sort of," said Franny. "Do you have any matches?" Ida raised an eyebrow.

"I don't want to make a fire." Franny felt her cheeks grow hot. "I like to build things for my dolls," she explained.

"Oh, well in that case, you can use these, they're not strike-anywheres." Ida gave her a box of wooden kitchen matches. "Henry has scraps of wood in the garage, no doubt. Ye might ask him for some. Now, don't be lookin' so bashful. Henry won't growl. He's the kindest man in the world." Suddenly Ida bit her lip and Franny saw that Ida's cheeks were pink too.

The garage was on the opposite side of the turnaround circle from the house. Once it had been the carriage house. Henry lived upstairs, but his apartment seemed separate and

57

private. Last night, through the window that was half hidden by the old wisteria vine, Franny had seen him reading.

Now Henry was mending a section of rain gutter at his workbench. His elderly English setter, Lady, slept in the shade near the open doorway. When Franny reached down to pat her, the dog jerked in surprise, and Franny noticed that her eyes were covered with a haze of white film. Lady got stiffly to her feet, looked in Franny's direction without really seeing her, and waved her feathery tail.

Forgetting her shyness, Franny crouched down to stroke the old dog's silky head. "You're a pretty girl, aren't you?" she said to Lady. Henry straightened up and smiled a slow half smile that seemed to start in his boots, it took so long to reach the one corner of his mouth where it lingered. Franny looked at him curiously. Papa was right. There was something about the way Henry's brown hair was parted, but wouldn't lie quite flat, the way his ears stuck out just a little, the skinniness of his neck, and the bigness of his Adam's apple that made him look like a boy, even though there were small lines at the corners of his mouth and oldness in his eyes. She stood up again. "Do you have any little pieces of wood you don't need?" she asked quickly.

"Yup," said Henry. He pulled a box out from under the workbench and let her sort through it. Franny liked that Henry didn't seem to feel that very much conversation was needed. "Want these?" He offered her a small hammer and a jar of nails. Franny nodded and took them. Then he saw her looking at a cigar box full of odds and ends of junk. Without a word, he dumped its contents into another box and handed that to her as well.

"Thanks," said Franny. Her arms were nearly full, but she managed to give Lady another pat before she left. It was funny. Without saying much of anything at all, Franny felt as if Henry was sort of a friend.

———◆———

THEY BEGAN BUILDING. TAMARACK USED NO OTHER TOOL but his rose-thorn knife, whittling pegs and boring holes with it, yet he was a skilled carpenter. Franny did the hardest part for him, lifting his lumber into the tree. Her fingers felt stiff and clumsy. She tried to follow his directions, but mostly she, Iris, and Meadowsweet fetched and carried or held things while Tamarack lashed them into place with bits of string, or pegged them, using a pebble for a hammer. Occasionally, he showed Franny where he wanted a nail or two driven for extra strength.

Franny found it difficult to hold the nails. Several times, she dropped them. She bit her lip and concentrated, ignoring the pulling of the tender new skin between her thumb and forefinger. It also hurt to clench her palm around the handle of the hammer, even with the protection of the bandage. She worked on making her fingertips come together to hold the nails, but still she would drop them and have to hunt them on the ground. Iris sent Meadowsweet for a comfrey leaf from the garden and rubbed juice from it onto Franny's hands, saying, "Never mind if they ask why your bandages are green. This will help." By lunchtime they had a sturdy platform, the size of a tea tray, in place.

All through the afternoon they worked. Meadowsweet and her mother sat on a low, mossy stone tying up bundles of grass with colored embroidery thread meant for Franny's sampler. They were making thatching. Franny and Tamarack built walls and put up rafters. By the time the first firefly winked on and off, they had Tamarack and Iris's bedroom finished. Franny placed a lovely tuft of moss, peeled from the roots of the tree, in one corner so that they would have a bed to sleep on that night.

By the next evening, Meadowsweet's own room was finished, as well as a combination kitchen/sitting room. Each had a porch with a railing around it. When it came time to make the rope ladders, Tamarack got the string all tangled up and muttered some things that sounded like they might have been swear words, so the tedious job of knotting string around the matchsticks was mostly left to the womenfolk. Henry's cigar box became a solarium/observatory perched stoutly in a crotch high in the crown of the tree. Franny wished that she were tiny enough to sit there in the evening with the Tamarack family, watching for falling stars. "It's just like looking into a deep ocean full of little sparkling fish, and then suddenly, one jumps," Meadowsweet whispered from her seat next to Franny's ear on her pillow one night.

Every night Meadowsweet climbed up through the ivy to visit with Franny for a few minutes before bed. Without her tiny friend, Franny knew that she would have felt very alone and that her thoughts would have turned to sad things, things that couldn't be undone. Meadowsweet must have known it too. As it was, they giggled about the way Mrs. Stark's stomach sometimes made noises, or the way her corset creaked when she bent over the stove.

Sometimes Meadowsweet would wind her arms around her drawn-up knees and sing a little wordless water sprite song. Franny would close her eyes and see pictures of waterfalls and ferny pools, or perhaps an underwater world of sun rays slanting down through waving lake weeds to golden sand below. When she opened her eyes again, it would be morning. The soft June air would be lifting and moving the curtains at the window, and Franny would be in a hurry to get out to the garden and the mulberry tree.

If Grandmother, working among her roses, noticed Franny coming and going from an opening between the drooping branches of the little tree, she didn't show it, but kept right on with her work. Sometimes Franny read a book for long, pleasant hours, but mostly she played with Meadowsweet and her family.

One afternoon, when Franny ducked into the shadow world under the mulberry branches, she noticed something in a crotch between two branches. Had a squirrel left it there? She looked closer. It was a clump of burdocks . . . no, it was a basket fashioned out of dried burdocks all stuck together, a funny little basket with a handle! It was lined with mint leaves and filled with wild strawberries.

Tamarack, Meadowsweet, and Iris gathered around. Meadowsweet seized a berry in her two hands and began greedily eating the ruby-colored fruit. Tamarack took out his knife and sliced one in two, offering half to Iris. Franny popped one into her mouth. It melted like candy on her tongue. Then there was no holding back or being polite. In no time at all, the basket was empty and they were all sucking the last taste of June sunshine and robin song from pink fingertips.

"You see," she whispered to the Tamarack family, "the folk of the garden are welcoming you. They are glad you have come."

The next day, Franny discovered a table constructed from a small piece of slate set on spools placed on the porch outside the main hut. On it had been carefully arranged a hickory-nut bowl full of tender new wintergreen leaves.

"I'm sure I don't know how it got here," said Iris, laughing, "but it's very kind of someone." The little snippets of leaves, with their delicious taste, reminded Franny of walking in the woods with her papa and nibbling wintergreen together.

The garden fairies, for Franny and Meadowsweet were certain that's who they were, continued leaving gifts: a smooth, white quartz pebble, a little string of beads made from twisted-up rose petals, a robin's egg shell full of water with a minute bouquet of bluets in it. Each was carefully placed in some part of the castle where Franny and the Tamarack family would find it.

"They are coming," Franny breathed as she carefully helped Meadowsweet arrange the tiny blue flowers in their eggshell vase. "They are very shy, but they're coming and they want to help!"

Chapter Eight ⌒

ONCE THE TREE HOUSE WAS LIVABLE, IT WAS TIME TO LOOK for the kingfisher's feather. Franny and her friends explored: upstairs, downstairs, cellar, attic, garden. Trolls rarely left their dark, wet homes under bridges, but they were tricky in a thick-headed sort of way. They *could* have crept into the house and hidden the feather in some cubbyhole that no one would think to look in. Anyway, the hunting was fun.

This place was so different from Mama's tidy house in Cambridge, or Nana DiCrista's fancy one. You could tell that an old person lived here because everything was neat and quiet, yet the big house was filled with collections and relics from years gone by—all those things that Nana called dead things. Whenever Mrs. Stark encountered Franny exploring, the housekeeper sniffed and gave her a look, but usually said nothing. Still it made Franny uncomfortable to think that anywhere and at any time Mrs. Stark might appear and scowl at her. Other than that, no one seemed to mind Franny's rambling.

In the parlor, before the fireplace, lay the great Kodiak bearskin rug. The bear's head and paws were still attached. It had been mounted with its own teeth, but given a new pink plaster tongue and gums. The lips were curled back in a thrilling snarl.

When Tamarack caught sight of the bear's gaping mouth, he drew his sword with one hand, and shoved Iris and Meadowsweet up a chair leg with the other. His face was grim. Iris took Meadowsweet firmly by the hand, and, tugging with all her strength, fluttered up to the safety of a curtain rod with her, refusing to come down. But once Tamarack saw that the bear was truly dead, he swaggered over, placed a hand on one of the frightful teeth, and peered into the gaping pink cave behind it.

"Sorry, Meadowsweet, no feather here. Come down, my love, the monster is dead. There's nothing to fear."

"I wouldn't dream of it, I don't even want to look at it."

"Oh, please, Mama. That old bear's as dead as a stump," begged Meadowsweet, her cheeks flushed with the unexpected treat of flying.

When Iris finally agreed to come down, Tamarack took her for a promenade all the way around the monster, stopping at each paw to examine the huge, curving claws. Iris was fascinated in spite of herself.

The bear's thick brown fur was warm in the patch of sunlight that made its way through the opening in the drapes. It smelled musky, almost alive. Franny knelt and smoothed the glossy hairs, feeling the denseness of the downy underfur. Then she lay down on the bear's back and stroked his head, as if he were a huge dog.

Meadowsweet took hold of the edge of an ear and scrambled to the top of the head. The fur here was slick and smooth. She pulled her skirt around her knees and slid, laughing, down into the shaggy shoulder fur. Then she waded through it, as if it were a field of tall grass, climbed up, and slid again.

Franny and the Tamarack family searched nearly every inch of the house for the kingfisher's feather. Stuffed birds peered and preened from the most unexpected places. Each had to be carefully examined for a small slate-colored feather that didn't belong to it. On a table in the upstairs hall, next to the grandfather clock, stood a great horned owl. He held a coiling garter snake forever in his talons while his huge yellow glass eyes followed, unblinking, no matter what corner of the hallway Franny stood in. She tried it, first from the landing, then from the corner near Grandmother's bedroom door, then from the beginning of the hallway to the servants' rooms over the kitchen. Each time the eyes found her and she shuddered. She couldn't help looking over her shoulder to see if Mrs. Stark was watching.

Franny tiptoed down the dark upstairs hallway and into each of the empty bedrooms. Sliding open a desk drawer in one room, she found a clutter of papers and junk, but no feather. She peeked into a dusty closet. On the shelves were several large flat boxes. She climbed on a chair and carefully lifted them down.

They contained a shell collection on cotton batting. Shells, still smelling and singing of faraway coral beaches: pink and white, mottled brown, luminous and sleek. They were neatly arranged with tiny paper labels glued to them. Franny turned each one over to read the delicate writing, but found no feather. The interior of the great heart cockle was salmon pink. "A bathtub!" Meadowsweet giggled, and climbed right in.

"Mind you don't crumple your new skirt, Meadowsweet," fussed Iris. She was busy stacking half a dozen tiny shells with lilac and lemon markings. "Ooh, lovely—soup bowls! Franny, be a dear and carry them back to the castle for me."

Another day, they explored the attic. On shelves under the eaves, they found a rock collection. The brittle labels had the same feathery writing. Franny whispered the names to herself: "Tourmaline: Harvard Quarry, Maine; Lepidolite: Telluride, Colorado; Iron Pyrite: Butte, Montana . . ." The sound of her own hushed voice seemed loud in the silent attic. There was no feather here. The rocks smelled old and forgotten. She remembered Nana's words, "She collects every dead thing under the sun. . . ."

"Are rocks dead?" she asked, turning to Iris.

"What do you think?" Iris said, lifting one eyebrow.

Franny blew the dust from them. A cloud of tiny specks swirled in the patch of sunlight that came through the small round attic window. Now the crystals glowed lavender, pink, and green. A tawny stone, flecked with black, gleamed like the hide of a sleeping leopard. Rainbow glints flashed from the little pyramid shapes in the chunk of pyrite.

It was strange. Most people would say that rocks were not living things, but Franny found that she couldn't think of them as dead either. They were part of the living world of rain, sun, and wind.

"I think," she said slowly, trying to puzzle it out, "that maybe . . . in some really deep, old, rocky kind of way . . . *they are alive.*"

There were other shelves filled with stacks of curious-looking, flat wooden boxes. Franny wanted to open some of them, but just then she heard a heavy tread on the stairs, and Mrs. Stark's head appeared in the stairwell opening. She fixed Franny with a dull, pale eye. "You are living proof that a child needs governing. I do not know what your grandmother is thinking, allowing you to your own devices. You might be doing something useful, like working on that sampler your Grandmother DiCrista sent. In my day, little ladies spent afternoons with their needlework, not inviting the devil's prompting with idleness."

Reluctantly, Franny left the attic.

OFTEN WHEN FRANNY LOOKED OUT HER WINDOW IN THE morning, she would see Grandmother striding back across the pasture, bird glasses around her neck, with perhaps some flowers, a clump of moss, or a bird's nest in her hand. Franny thought she walked fast for an old lady. Later, if her study door was open, Franny would see her at the table by the window with the morning's specimens laid out before her, poring over them with a magnifying glass, flipping pages in books, or placing leaves and blossoms between pages of a large leather-bound press. Sometimes she might look up and smile a funny little apologetic smile at Franny, but she never asked her to come and see what she was doing.

Mealtimes had not improved much. Franny thought that in some ways they both tried, but she knew that for her, it was easier to stay behind the glass wall that seemed to separate them. She wondered if maybe it was easier for Grandmother to stay behind her side of that glass wall too.

One Saturday morning Grandmother said, "Why don't you come to my bird lecture with me this morning? It's on the structure of wings and feathers—how they fly—and should be very interesting. Perhaps you'd enjoy it."

"I don't know," Franny answered uncertainly, but she could feel Meadowsweet inside the basket pounding with frustration. "Well, maybe," she said.

Before she got all the way upstairs to her room, Meadowsweet had the lid off the basket. "Franny, we *have* to go," she squeaked. "If I could find out how birds fly, it wouldn't matter if I never found the kingfisher's feather. I could use any old feathers we found lying around!"

So Franny went. Henry drove them in to Cambridge in the Cadillac and waited for them outside. The lecture was in a chalk-dusty classroom in an old brick building on the Harvard campus. It was hot. The starched collar of Franny's blouse stuck to the back of her neck. She tugged at her stockings, wishing she could peel them off and throw them in a heap somewhere. She picked at the tender new pink skin on her fingers while the man in the rumpled suit droned on, pointing at charts of seagull skeletons. Once, she stole a look at Grandmother. The old woman's eyes were bright, and she was listening as if the man were saying something very exciting just to her.

Franny fidgeted with the handle of the basket. When the professor unrolled another chart, and she was sure Grandmother wouldn't notice, she lifted the lid for a moment and peeked inside. Meadowsweet puckered up her face at Franny like a winter crab apple. "I thought he was going to tell us how to fly," she hissed. Then her manner changed. *"The outer veins of the primary feathers are not symmetrical at the tips, but become more so at the base . . ."* she recited in a tiny nasal voice, mimicking the professor. She crossed her eyes at Franny. "BORING!" Franny grinned and closed the lid.

Franny didn't think she would come to the next Saturday morning lecture, but she had to admit that in her own stiff and hesitant way, Grandmother was trying. That evening she asked Franny to play checkers with her. The big old house had electric lighting, but it still seemed dark because Grandmother Morrow used only low-wattage light bulbs so that her house was no brighter than if it were still lighted only by oil and gas lamps. There were two table lamps in the parlor, their glass shades painted with delicate pink roses, but they made only pools of light surrounded by shadow.

Although she had a telephone, Grandmother seldom used it. "Mr. Bell, Mr. Edison, and Mr. Ford have achieved great wonders," she told Franny as she switched on the lights, "but it was a prettier world before them."

Mrs. Stark came in and set up the card table and chairs next to the bearskin rug. Franny sat down, kicked a slipper off, and buried the toes of her right foot in the bear's long, soft fur.

"Your move, Franny. You know, your father always used to beat me at checkers. Uncle George couldn't, but Arthur showed me no mercy. I just can't believe I'll never play checkers with him again."

Franny studied the checkerboard stonily and fingered the handle of the basket in her lap. Grandmother sighed.

"Franny, maybe you should try to talk about your papa," she said at last. "I know it hurts terribly to think of him being dead and never coming back, but Franny, there are so many good things to remember. Your papa wouldn't want you to be sad for so long."

Inside, Franny burned with anger. She did not want to

hear about this dead person. The moment dragged into minutes. Grandmother sat very straight in her chair.

"Franny?" Then Grandmother asked softly, "Tell me, child, what do you keep in the basket?"

Deliberately, Franny got up and walked up the stairs to her room, leaving her grandmother to put away the checker pieces.

Chapter Nine ～

AFTER THAT, FRANNY FOUND HERSELF AVOIDING GRAND-mother and turning toward Ida. The kitchen, if Mrs. Stark was elsewhere, was a pleasant place with more life in it than the rest of the house. It could be hot and tense in the late afternoons when Mrs. Stark was preparing the evening meal, but other times it was nice.

One day, Franny found herself helping Ida make bread at the kitchen table. She set her basket in a safe place on the counter by the sink while she washed her hands. She hadn't needed any bandages at all for a few days now. The burns were healed, but some of her fingers still didn't move the way they should. Ida showed her how to fold and stretch the ball of dough. At first Franny pushed awkwardly at it, frowning. She couldn't tell if her hands really hurt or if she was just re-membering how much they had hurt when her palms and fin-gers were covered with oozing blisters.

She could feel Ida watching her. Then Ida stepped behind her and put her own hands over Franny's. They felt warm and strong. Very gently, she helped Franny's hands go through the motions of kneading. "There now," she said. "Let the dough work your hands just as you work it. It's a lovely feeling. I've a notion that kneading bread dough is just the thing for them right now."

Franny felt something inside herself relax. She and Ida pushed and pulled in a rhythm, adding pinches of flour until the dough had lost its stickiness. Franny's hands didn't hurt now. It felt delicious to punch and squeeze and pull at the dough. It smelled yeasty and alive. She couldn't wait for the mouthwatering scent of it baking.

When Ida talked, something in her manner tugged at Franny's heart. It seemed almost as if Ida had once been hit hard in the pit of her stomach and never quite recovered her breath. She did not like America. As they worked the dough, she told why.

"There's no magic here, Franny, no little folk. No one speaks of them or sees them. It is a heartless land—but your grandmother is kind," she added quickly.

Franny nearly told her about Tamarack, Iris, and Meadowsweet listening from inside her basket at that very moment, but instead she said, "Tell me about Ireland."

Ida's eyes flickered. For a moment there was almost a light in them. "Well, 'tis green, but a richer green than you see here. So green . . . and there are rocks and walls, and hummocks so ancient, and yet *someone* put them there . . . and always something a bit strange, as if there were a whole world of unseen people. We call them the little folk: the fairies and leprechauns . . . If ever I put a saucer of milk on the door stoop nights, they'd be sure to sup it by morning."

"Have you tried it here?" Franny asked, wondering if garden fairies liked milk.

"Aye. It soured." Ida rose quickly and turned to the sink. Franny saw her hand brush at her eyes. She was crying. Ida's sadness made Franny ache inside. She wanted to tell her about the Tamarack family, she really did. But not just yet.

Ida showed Franny how to form the loaves and pat them into their pans. Then they set them on the warming shelf of the stove and covered them with a damp towel. They wiped the table clean again. Ida made them each a cup of tea, and then set a bowl of cherries in front of Franny, saying, " 'Tis too dreary a house for a young one all by her lonesome. You should be shouting and rollicking, not slippin' about with a long face and big eyes. Eat a bit and put some color in your cheeks."

They sat together at the kitchen table while the bread rose. Ida told Franny of the little house in Ireland, full of brothers and sisters, where she grew up. "We could see the peak of Croagh Patrick wreathed in mist from the kitchen window, and the island of Inishbofin from the front doorway, lying like a silver fish on the blue sea. There were the five of them to watch over, and me the oldest. Mother was in hospital nearly two years with osteomyelitis. That's infection of the bone. It took me months just to learn to say it. They thought the infection might be tuberculosis and we all might have it, but praise Mary, we didn't."

Franny bit into a ripe cherry. Knowing that Meadowsweet must be watching her hungrily, she dropped one in her pocket to give her later.

"We danced, you know," Ida continued. "I was the little mother, like Wendy, in your book about Peter Pan. Dad worked, and me little brothers and sister and I danced in the kitchen, like fairies bewitched. It's a wonder the wee folk didn't whist us all away! Nights, when Dad was home, I worked at the inn. . . ."

Then it was time to put the bread in the oven. "Why, you've eaten every one of those cherries!" exclaimed Ida as she brought the teacups to the sink. Franny smiled to herself. She knew very well that she'd left several cherries in the bowl. She hoped Meadowsweet wouldn't have a stomachache later. She thought about how good it had felt to squeeze the bread dough and feel that her hands were her own again. It had been nice hearing Ida's story, but Franny thought there must be more of it, something she wasn't telling. Something that was the reason for her sadness. At the same time Franny felt a little stab of guilt. Here she'd been having a pleasant morning, but it had been a long time to ignore the Tamarack family.

Chapter Ten ⤳

THE NEXT MORNING, GRANDMOTHER WAS NOT AT BREAK-
fast and Franny ate alone. As she left the dining room, she very
nearly bumped into Grandmother hurrying to her study, her
sweater still on and a tiny nest cradled carefully in both hands.

"Oh!" she said, looking up. Her cheeks were flushed and
her eyes very bright. Before Franny could even say "excuse
me," Grandmother continued, as if she could barely hold in
her excitement. "It's a golden crowned warbler's nest, child.
See how she made the little bower of feathers? Would you believe it? Audubon himself never found one. It was in one of the
blue spruces your grandfather planted. I got prickled pretty
badly, reaching for it. I've been watching it and this year it was
abandoned. See, it's a little rag-tag. I wouldn't want to take
one that was in use. But isn't it cunningly built?"

Franny looked at the nest and felt her heart start thumping quickly. She had never seen a bird's nest like this. It was a
neat, deep little construction of twigs, shredded bark, and
lichen no bigger than a teacup. The quite amazing thing about

it was that half a dozen downy feathers had been tucked upright into the rim so that they arched like a tiny canopy over the interior of the nest. Franny parted them with a careful fingertip to peer inside. It was lined with fine grasses, hair, and what looked like milkweed down. Didn't Grandmother realize? No bird had made this. Only the tiniest of hands could have been so clever.

"It's a fairy cradle," she said. Grandmother gave her an odd look, but didn't argue. Without thinking, Franny put her hand on Grandmother's to have a closer look. Her grandmother's manner suddenly changed. She stiffened and a look almost like pain crossed her face. She closed her mouth, compressing her lips, and looked down at the floor. Franny took her hand away. She could feel the glass wall between them again. What was it that made Grandmother act like that? She thought of Papa's words, "I think something in life hurt her once."

After a moment, Grandmother said, "Well, it will be a nice addition to my collection," but her tone was flat. The excitement was gone and she spoke almost as if Franny weren't even there. Franny looked after her in wonder and not a little anger. Well, it *was* a fairy's cradle. It had to be. Why did Grandmother insist that such a magical thing was made by some stupid bird?

Franny went out to the garden, climbed into her tree, and leaned her head back, letting her legs swing. Sometimes she felt as if Papa were right around the corner, just in another room, or about to run lightly up the steps, toss his hat into a chair, and say, "Ugh, I'm glad to be out of that office." Then he would say, "Where's my fairy princess?" meaning Franny.

She remembered the smothery office in Boston, where Mama had taken her once on an October day that made her cheeks feel like pincushions. They had stepped out of the sweep and crisp of wind and fallen leaves into a strange, still place. Voices murmured in low tones, sometimes a telephone jangled, and in the background, a typewriter pecked endlessly, like a bird in a cage. Her feet echoed on the floor, and she couldn't breathe properly in the musty air. She had watched one of the flies trapped on the windowsill and felt sorry for Papa to have to spend his days here, at his desk, when the frost fairies were painting the world fire colors and the sky was as blue as a lake.

Uncle Edward and Uncle George worked here too. Each brother had his own office with gold letters on the frosted glass of the door. But her uncles seemed happier than Papa. They didn't stare out the window for long moments the way Papa did.

———◆———

THERE WAS STILL THE BARN TO EXPLORE. IT WOULDN'T hurt to look for the kingfisher's feather there. It stood a little way below the house, beside a stone wall and a row of big white pines. Henry was at work in the pasture out back, replacing a section of fence. He leaned on his shovel and smiled his half smile at Franny. Lady got up stiffly from her dog nest in the grass with a soft, friendly woof.

"Where are Bobby Burns and Marigold?" asked Franny.

Henry nodded toward the barn. "Inside. They was snuffling my pockets and nuzzling my neck, and Bobby was trying awful hard to step in this post hole." It was a long speech for Henry. As if surprised at it himself, he snapped his mouth shut and went back to work with his shovel.

Franny managed to slide the big green barn door open enough to squeeze inside, and stood a moment, letting her eyes get used to the dimness. Sunlight, slanting through cracks between the weathered boards, lighted up the dusty, soaring spaces over her head. It was very quiet. She took a deep breath of timothy, alfalfa, dust, and old leather, mingled with horse and cow smells.

Bobby and Marigold looked over their stall doors curiously. Franny stood still. Mama and Papa had always ridden the trolley cars in Cambridge. They didn't have an automobile or a carriage. She had patted delivery horses, ridden in other people's carriages, and even ridden the Van Reusens' pony a few times, but still, she felt cautious.

The old horse nodded his head impatiently, as if asking why on earth she didn't rub his neck. Marigold swung her heavy head and stared at Franny with enormous brown eyes.

"Come on, Franny, I dare you," teased Meadowsweet, who was now perched on Franny's shoulder—so she put out her hand and touched first Bobby's velvet nose and then Marigold's wet one. The cow's great pink tongue slid out and tasted Franny's hand. Franny drew it back quickly with a half-scared laugh.

Together, Franny and Meadowsweet climbed the ladder into the hayloft. There were lots of pigeon and swallow feathers scattered here and there in the hay. Franny sighed in frustration. "How in the world are we going to find one tiny gray feather?" she asked.

"It's magic, Franny," Meadowsweet reminded her. "You have to keep believing we'll find it."

They came back down just as Mr. B was coming in. He had a long Italian name with lots of *i*'s and *o*'s in it, but everybody just called him Mr. B. He poured a measure of grain into Bobby's feed box. Impatiently, Marigold craned her neck around the partition. "Now, don't you be rolling your eyes," he said with a chuckle. "You'll get your breakfast too." He spoke to them as if they were little children, rubbing their necks with his knotted hands. The gray stubble on his chin jumped as he spoke.

Franny lingered, watching Bobby eat. There was something about the softness of his muzzle and the kindness of his eye that made her want to put her arms around his neck. He was even better than the bearskin, because he was alive. His bay coat was sprinkled with white hairs, and his back was slightly swayed, but there was still an arch to his neck that told her he had once been a handsome carriage horse.

Mr. B let Franny brush Bobby. "He's just itchin' for a good all-over groomin'. He's a horse that used to enjoy his day's beautifyin' as much as his work."

She stretched on tiptoe to reach the broad back. The currycomb was all right because it had a strap that fit across the back of her hand and most of the work came from her elbow, but she kept dropping the brush. Finally, out of breath, her pinafore dusty and her knuckles black, she inspected her work. Bobby looked much better. He even seemed to arch his neck a little more.

"There, now, that's the first time I've seen the little miss smile," Mr. B said to Bobby. The elderly horse rubbed against Franny's shoulder as if he were pleased. "My old eyes are getting bad," Mr. B said to Franny. "Would you want to hunt eggs for me tomorrow?"

She nodded. Where there were chickens there would be lots of feathers. It wasn't until Franny was hopping along the flagstone path in the garden that she realized she had left Meadowsweet in the basket on top of the grain. She dashed back to the barn.

"Let's see . . ." said Meadowsweet crossly when Franny peeked into the basket, "spiders, snakes, barn cats, and don't forget weasels. . . . I'm sure Mama wouldn't have minded me walking back up to the house by myself."

"Oh, Meadowsweet, I'm sorry," said Franny. For the second time in just more than a day, she felt the guilt of forgetting the Tamarack family. What was the matter with her?

MEADOWSWEET PROVED TO BE VERY CLEVER AT FINDING eggs. She even slipped under the ruffled red feathers of a stubborn old biddy sitting in a corner behind an empty barrel, and came out huffing, pushing an egg that was almost hot, it was so new. They filled Franny's basket, and Meadowsweet rode on top of the eggs as if it were a wagon load of smooth brown boulders, but they found no tiny gray feather among all the glossy red ones dropped by the hens.

Suddenly Franny heard mewing from the toolshed. There in a box of rags under the workbench was one of the barn cats with a newborn litter of kittens. The mother cat slipped away when Franny crouched to look. Even with their eyes closed, the kittens were lovely. Meadowsweet pulled a calico, no bigger than herself, into her lap. The kitten flailed its paws and turned its head, seeking its mama. Franny thought of cuddling a lion cub. "Please, please, please, mayn't I have just one?" begged Meadowsweet. "We could build her a cage and keep her in the tree house."

Franny had to be very firm. "Meadowsweet, you know how afraid your mama is of cats. Besides, they're too young now. They can't leave their mother or climb trees yet."

"That they are, but ain't they purty, missy?"

Franny caught her breath as Mr. B stumped in and set down a roll of wire and some cutters on the workbench. She looked up at him in confusion. She knew he couldn't see Meadowsweet, but what must he think?

THE NICE THING ABOUT THE BARN WAS THAT THERE WAS no Mrs. Stark to watch her. Whenever Franny went there, Bobby nickered happily, for he soon learned that there might be lumps of sugar, sneaked from the dining room sugar bowl, in her pocket. To Meadowsweet, he was like a great moving hillside with plenty of fur to grasp for climbing about. She danced like a tiny circus lady on his broad hindquarters while he munched hay and Franny curried him.

"Now, you come and help get these burdocks out of his mane," Franny whispered sternly, but Meadowsweet just shrugged her shoulders and twirled on one foot.

Bobby would let Franny walk up to him in the pasture. She braided buttercups into his forelock in tiny fairy braids. And one day, when he was cropping the grass next to the fence, Franny climbed up and slid onto his back. Bobby's head went up and he twitched his shoulder muscles in surprise, but she whispered to him and stroked his neck until he went back to grazing. Franny sat there, dreaming in the sunshine, until suddenly she felt an insistent yanking on a strand of her hair.

"Ow! Meadowsweet, stop it!" she cried.

Meadowsweet stood on her shoulder with her arms crossed bossily. "You're getting sidetracked, Franny. At this rate I'll be a grandma before I get to fly."

Chapter Eleven ∼

FRANNY AND MEADOWSWEET WENT BACK TO EXPLORING.
"Maybe you should try to forget about the kingfisher's gift
and just enjoy the summer," Iris suggested gently to her
daughter, but Meadowsweet would not give up. One afternoon, poking into the tangle of overgrown rhododendron,
laurel, and hemlock in the middle of the turnaround, she and
Franny discovered a mossy garden pool at the base of a single
old white pine. The hidden pipe feeding the pool was half
plugged and rusty, but still dripped bright, cool drops and
kept it filled. With the jungle of neglected shrubbery as a
screen, the little clearing seemed like its own world. Meadowsweet was into the pool in a flash, giggling with joy. Franny
pulled off her shoes and stockings and dangled her feet in the
water. The days were getting sticky and the nights sweltering.
She looked at the twisted roots of the tree. What a wonderful
weekend place this would make for Tamarack's family!

Then she saw, with a prickle at the back of her neck, something from her books, something that she had once tried to

make herself, a thing that Ida had said was to be found only in Ireland. A ring of mushrooms grew in a space between the roots of the old tree. *A fairy ring.* Something, someone . . . had left an acorn top on one of the mushrooms . . . a cup? Did the garden fairies visit this place?

———•———

AT BEDTIME IDA WAS BRUSHING FRANNY'S HAIR. HER FINgers worked patiently and gently. "It's like me sister Eileen's hair, full of fairy knots now, but 'twill be glossy like a horse's tail when you're older. Soon ye'll be a young lady and wearing it up."

At the mention of fairies, Franny smiled, remembering the afternoon's discovery. She turned to Ida, her eyes glowing with joy. "I found the most wonderful thing today! In the middle of the bushes in the turnaround, there's a huge old pine tree with big twisty roots, and in the space between the roots there's a *fairy ring*!"

Ida's hand with the hairbrush in it stopped in midair. There was a flicker in Ida's dark eyes—almost like joy. Then she was thoughtful again. "Well, now," she said slowly, "it maybe is and maybe isn't."

But the next morning, when Franny led Ida, with her skirts tucked up, through the thicket, they found only blown and blackened remains of fungi. Yet they *were* in a ring. There was no doubt about that. Ida clucked her tongue. " 'Tis surely a nice secret spot," she said quietly.

Franny began helping Tamarack's family build a cottage they called Lakeholm out of twigs and bark at the base of the great pine, beside the little pool. Here, under this arching root, was Meadowsweet's bedroom. Over there, where it curved again, was the master bedroom. The floors were paved with little flat stones, and it had a roof of twigs. She peeled velvety swatches of moss from a dead branch for carpeting. She hunted for little round moss cushions for seats and beds. Here was the banquet hall, there the throne room for granting audiences (for the local fairies might have tributes to offer and disputes to settle), and here, where water trickled from the pipe into the pool, was the kitchen and scullery.

"Oh, Tamarack, must she swim?" fretted Iris as Meadowsweet fluttered about for hours, like a tiny mermaid, in the mossy depths of the pool.

"I'm afraid we can't go against her nature, my love," answered Tamarack. "But if it's any comfort to you, there are no fish in there. She'll come to no harm. We might as well have a dip ourselves."

Iris shuddered. On particularly hot days, she would dabble her toes, but she would not swim. Tamarack paddled and kicked like a frog, but Meadowsweet surfaced, laughing for joy whenever her papa dove in to join her.

———•———

GRANDMOTHER CONTINUED TO BE DISTANT. IT WAS ALmost as if she didn't or couldn't quite see Franny. She was not unkind, she just seemed wrapped in her world of flowers and birds. Sometimes she would appear to see Franny for a moment and start to speak, but then she would catch herself, as if remembering the mysterious glass between them. Other times she made polite conversation in a way that Franny knew was meant to be kind, but always seemed forced—as if Franny were some strange little girl visiting and not her own granddaughter.

Letters began arriving from Mama, looking terribly important with their foreign stamps. But they said nothing, really.

Dearest Franny,

It was a long voyage. Your Nana and I were quite ill the first few days and stayed strictly in our cabin. On the third day we ventured out and took some air on the deck. The sea was rather monotonous, there being so very much of it. Some of our companions exclaimed at the lighting and atmosphere and seemed quite charmed with the prospect of nothing but water all around us, but I found it gray and dreary. . . .

. . . London is very entertaining and respectable. We have been to the theater twice. Your grandparents have several friends here, and I have been introduced all around. I think they are eager for me to become friendly with an American gentleman, Mr. Adams. He

is very pleasant and quite a good dancer. He says
comical things to make me laugh and I am sure you
would like him. . . .

. . . Nana told me that the rest has done me good
and that I look as young as when your poor papa and
I were married. I hardly think so, but we did buy an
evening gown during our stay in Paris. It is of mauve
satin, trimmed with lace and velvet ribbon, and
designed by Poiret himself. I think it exactly suits
me. Nana assures me that enough time has passed
and I need not wear black, which does not become
me at all. . . .

Mama had given her a box of white stationery with her ini-
tials embossed at the top in curly letters, but Franny didn't
write back. Instead she took out a sheet and wrote to Papa.

Dear Papa,
How are you? I am fine, but I miss you.

She stared at the words a long time. Then slowly, she
began writing again.

Is it lonely by yourself? Are you having lots of time
to make stories with Mama and me away? I am
writing at your old desk. Grandmother thought I
would like to stay in your room, and I do. Tamarack
and his family are fine, although Queen Iris misses
the home castle some.

Franny found she was writing more quickly now, almost as if her pen were moving by itself.

They have a lakeside cottage under the roots of the big pine by the driveway here, and a tree house castle in the weeping mulberry—just like Falcon's Nest in Swiss Family Robinson. They found some small boards in the garage. Iris insisted they have a ladder like a proper tree house, so we made one out of string and kitchen matches. I forgot to put the string back in the drawer. Mrs. Stark was awful mad when she missed it.

Iris and Meadowsweet spend a lot of time in Grandmother's rose garden making dresses. There are twenty different kinds of roses, and Iris wants a dress made out of each. She keeps having tempers at Meadowsweet, because Meadowsweet goes to the barn to ride Bobby Burns and comes home with all the nice rose smell covered with barn smell and most of her petals torn.

And Papa, the funniest thing happened yesterday when Meadowsweet was snooping in Mrs. Stark's coat pocket. Mrs. Stark had to suddenly go out to market because she'd forgotten to order the Sunday roast and she wouldn't trust Henry to pick it out. She was in a positive fury and made Henry drive very fast, and there was Meadowsweet in her pocket because there'd been no time to escape. Everything was all right until Mrs. Stark bought a packet of cinnamon hearts and stuffed them in on top of Meadowsweet. Of course Meadowsweet ate one, but it was too hot for her and she began to choke, and Mrs. Stark thought there was a mouse in her pocket and slapped at it until she spilled the candies all over the floor right in the store, and Meadowsweet just barely scrambled up into her hat that looks like a Hubbard squash and hid there all the way home smelling the awful sour milk smell of Mrs. Stark's hair. . . .

When Franny had finished the letter, she put her head down on her arms for a few minutes and closed her eyes. Then she carefully sealed and addressed it with the Cambridge address, put one of the stamps Mama had given her on it, took it downstairs, and placed it in the letter holder just outside the front door.

THE NEXT MORNING, FRANNY AWOKE VERY EARLY TO A tiny sound, like puffs of wind on water. It was just beginning to be light outside. Meadowsweet was sitting on her window ledge with Stripesy in her lap, her face buried in her pet's fur. She was crying. Franny slipped out of bed, padded across the floor, and knelt by the window.

"Meadowsweet, what's the matter?" she asked softly. She looked out through the window at the mulberry tree, trying to see if something had happened. Then she noticed a flicker of pale emerald green hovering over Grandmother's peony bed, and knew. As she watched there was another flash of green, higher up, as the rising sun caught a pair of wings. Iris and Tamarack were flying together, when they thought Meadowsweet was still asleep.

There didn't seem to be much to say. Franny put out her hand and Meadowsweet climbed into it. For what seemed like a long time, Franny held her gently cupped against her cheek. She could feel the shuddering of Meadowsweet's tiny shoulders, like the flutter of a grasshopper kicking against her fingers. It was strange. Here she felt closer than ever to Meadowsweet and her family, and it was such fun to write to Papa telling about their adventures, yet every now and then she could forget about them completely. Why was that? After a bit, she felt Meadowsweet grow quiet and heard her say, "I'm all right now."

Franny set her back on the window ledge. "We're *going* to find your feather, Meadowsweet. There are places we haven't looked yet. Remember, we never finished looking up in the attic after Mrs. Stark found us that time."

The little water sprite nodded and wiped her eyes on the hem of her lady's-smock pinafore. "Don't tell Mama and Papa that I saw them or that I cried," she whispered. "They never fly if they think I'll see them, and I know they must miss it. It's not their fault I can't do it." Then she suddenly kicked her feet at the ivy leaves that crowded around the window ledge. "Sometimes I hate being a water sprite," she said fiercely.

———•———

IDA ALWAYS HAD A SMILE AND A NOD FOR FRANNY, BUT Franny could tell she was sad—bitterly sad down to her bones. She went about her work, strong arms scrubbing and sweeping, but her heart seemed dead. It made Franny think of how the strings of a violin couldn't ring clearly if you didn't press your fingers down all the way. Something wasn't right. Often Ida sighed or paused to stand, staring at something that wasn't there. Somehow Franny felt that Ida should rightfully be singing, that something was keeping the music from coming out.

Franny had never seen black hair with freckled skin. She always thought freckles went with red or blonde, or even her own no-special-color, brownish hair. After thinking about it, she decided Ida's coloring was exotic and nice. Her hair snaked in a thick braid down her back, or was sometimes twisted into loops at her nape.

By contrast, Mrs. Stark's hair was raked tightly into a knot on top of her head. A fringe of gray frizz didn't do much to soften the pasty hardness of her face. She didn't exactly look sick, but then she didn't exactly look well either. Her hair swept up one way and her bosom swept out the other, like a broad, shapeless buttress. Franny wondered how she could have so very much bosom and yet not look womanly at all. Her backside was big and bony, almost like Marigold's, but Marigold was soft and pretty even if she was a cow.

Franny wondered if Mrs. Stark had ever liked anybody. She disapproved of Franny and she clearly disliked Henry. But for Ida she reserved an opinion that Franny could only think of as poisonous. There didn't seem to be a reason, except that Franny had known people before—some of the children at school, and a few grown-ups—who seemed to hate a person for the way they talked, or the color of their skin, or even where they came from. She had heard people say bad things about Irish people before.

One morning Ida was busy baking a second batch of muffins to suit Mrs. Stark. The housekeeper was braiding Franny's hair so tightly it hurt. She said to Franny, in her raspy voice, "I wouldn't have asked a starving cur to eat those muffins! There's a right way and a wrong way to do everything, and the only thing you can trust about the Irish is that they'll do it wrong. Now, hurry along, miss. Little ladies must learn to be prompt for meals."

After Mrs. Stark went back downstairs, Meadowsweet popped over the window ledge. "Papa's helping Mama make raspberry wine, but they said I could come play with you. Franny, it was Mrs. Stark's own fault about the muffins. She's the one who told Ida not to use so much baking powder, and then said that they weren't done and that she should cook them longer!" Meadowsweet grinned. "I was snitching raisins. I brought you one."

"Thanks," said Franny, putting the single small fruit in her mouth. She would have liked a few more, but was glad Meadowsweet hadn't tried to climb up through the ivy with an armful. She tugged on a shoe and began buttoning it. "You know, it must be easy for Mrs. Stark," she said. "There isn't any 'maybe' or 'in a minute' or 'that's good enough.' It's either right or wrong, black or white. In her world there's no pinkish purple or pale gold."

Meadowsweet put one hand on her hip, made a sour mouth, and rolled her eyes. *"Little ladies do not speak unless spoken to,"* she said, imitating Mrs. Stark's voice so that she sounded like a tiny rusty hinge. She shook a finger at Franny. *"Little ladies take baths at six o'clock and go directly to bed— preferably with the sun blazing and birds still chirping!"* Franny began to giggle. Meadowsweet continued, warming to her audience. *"Little ladies must have their fingernails scrubbed and cut to the quick so that they are sore for at least two days. They do not tear their stockings climbing trees. They do not put too much butter on their bread or too much sugar on their oatmeal! Such indulgence is not suited to the digestion of a child!"*

Franny had to clap a hand over her mouth to stifle her laughter. With the other she tried to tug the last button of her right shoe through its buttonhole with the silver buttonhook. "What about Mrs. Stark's little habits?" she asked Meadowsweet. "Whenever Grandmother or I get up from a chair, she swoops over to straighten the antimacassars. I've seen her go into the parlor just to tug at them, even if they're not crooked. It's like she just *has* to do it. And the teacups have to be hung just so, six going one way and six going the other. And she always mutters when she dusts Grandmother's birds, as if they were nasty. Sometimes I feel like she thinks Grandmother and I are the dirtiest people in the world and that we just try to mess up her tidy house on purpose."

Franny finally managed to fasten the last button and began working on the other shoe. "I think I hate it most the way she scolds Ida for not folding towels the right way or slicing beans straight instead of at a slant, or some stupid little thing that doesn't even matter. And then there's the *look*. Did you ever see anyone look at a person the way Mrs. Stark does? It's like she's trying to find something wrong with you. She starts at your feet and looks you up and down until you start feeling as though you must have see-through skin or something. But she smiles like peaches at Grandmother." Franny made a fake smile and spoke though her nose, *"Certainly, Mrs. Morrow! I'll see that it's done right away, Mrs. Morrow!"* Now Meadowsweet was laughing so hard that she snorted a little snort, like a mouse sneeze, through her nose.

They were late coming down for breakfast, and Mrs. Stark was waiting at the bottom of the stairs. Her eyes narrowed. Sure enough, it was the *look*. Franny's skin began to crawl. She could feel a little vibration from inside the basket. Meadowsweet was fairly humming with annoyance. As Franny reached the bottom stair, Mrs. Stark announced, as if Franny had been waiting for a verdict, "The reason you are knock-kneed is not so much that your legs are crooked, but that they are too fat."

Franny was stunned. She knew she was plain, but never in her life had she been called fat or knock-kneed. Later she climbed on the chair in her room to look at her legs in the mirror over the dresser. They were sturdy legs, yes, not slender like Meadowsweet's, but were they fat? She wished Papa were there to tell her. He would know. But Papa . . . She pushed the thought roughly away. As she climbed down from the chair, one of her shoe buttons caught on the little lace circle pinned to an arm of the chair. She started to straighten it and then stopped. On her way out to the garden, she stepped into the parlor and quickly rumpled the antimacassars on the sofa. Meadowsweet found a cobweb under a chair and stretched it across the top of one of the lampshades. After that, Franny began secretly to give the bits of lace on the furniture backs little twitches of her own. Again and again she tugged them out of place. Again and again Mrs. Stark yanked them straight. It was like a silent battle between the two of them.

"Sometimes I think there are demons in this house," seethed Mrs. Stark. "You just tell me how a cobweb can appear on a lamp I dusted not twenty-four hours ago." But Franny thought she fed on unpleasantness, like some sort of poisonous plant. Sometimes, on purpose, Franny turned a teacup around as she passed the china cupboard. She inched the drapes back to let in more sun and even tore her stocking on purpose, but she was always careful not to do too much lest Ida be the one who got in trouble.

Once Franny sneaked into Mrs. Stark's room in the wing over the kitchen. It was bare and uninviting. It felt somehow cooler than the other rooms in the house and had a faint sour smell. There was no way to know anything about the person who lived there because there was no knickknack on the shelf, book on the bedside table, or picture on the wall to give a clue. Only on the dresser was a row of medicines. Franny read the label on a tall bottle: "the best for dyspepsia, malassimilation of food, stomach disorders, general functional derangement, constipation, bilious headache, and female debility." Next to it, a tin read, "Dr. Worden's Female Pills, a Valuable Specific for Female Troubles and Nerve Difficulties." Franny didn't know what "female troubles" might be, but she guessed it might have something to do with babies. Mrs. Stark never talked about children, if she had any. She never even mentioned a Mr. Stark. Beside the tin of pills was a nearly empty jar of "Mother Helm's Powder, a Gentle, Never-Fail Daily Bowel Stimulant." That must be what Franny saw her stirring up in a glass sometimes if she came into the kitchen early.

Franny didn't exactly mean to snoop, but before she thought about it, she opened the top drawer. There, next to knitted stockings and undergarments that looked sturdy enough to girdle an elephant, were goodies—forbidden sweets "too rich for any child"—a box of chocolates, a striped bag of mints, and a tin of butter cookies. Just then Franny heard slow, heavy steps on the back stairs. Hurriedly she tried to close the drawer, but it jammed. She had just decided to leave it jammed and make a run for it when Mrs. Stark filled the doorway.

For the tiniest moment, there was a look on the woman's face as if she were the one who had been caught and not Franny. Then her face blackened with anger and she advanced on her employer's granddaughter, shaking a thick white finger at her. "It's not enough that you should poke and pry into every nook and cranny of your grandmother's rooms—and I never saying a word about such deceitful behavior in a child— but now I find you rifling through my personal things like some nasty little ferret!"

Franny ducked under a massive elbow and ran.

Chapter Twelve ⌒

ONE AFTERNOON, FRANNY CAME INTO THE HALL TO FIND Ida sweeping up clumps of mud that must have been tracked onto the rug when she'd run in from the garden. Ida was working quickly, looking over her shoulder, as if trying to do it before Mrs. Stark noticed. Franny realized suddenly that Ida was watching out for her. Later, when Franny dropped a glass on the kitchen floor, Ida actually took the blame while Franny's mouth hung open, waiting for Mrs. Stark's reaction.

"Dear me, it's careless I am today."

"Every day, miss," croaked Mrs. Stark, snapping her mouth open and shut like a box.

The thing that Franny wished about Ida was that she would be nicer to Henry. Anybody could see that Henry admired Ida, but he seemed tongue-tied around her. She hardly seemed to know he was there. He did little kindnesses for her but she didn't even seem to notice.

One morning, while Henry sat at the kitchen table drinking a cup of coffee, and Franny was squeezing lemons for lemonade by the sink, Ida climbed onto a chair to reach the pitcher from the top shelf. Mrs. Stark could have reached it, but Franny knew Ida couldn't have asked her. That afternoon Franny noticed a little wooden stool in the corner by the roller towel. It looked like it was made of new wood. Sometimes when Ida used the stool, there would be a funny look on her face, but she never said a word about it.

Once when a thunderstorm was blowing up, Franny saw Henry come in with the wicker basket full of dry clothes from the line just as Ida was heading out the door in a panic. She had to thank him then, but her eyes never looked up at his.

Another day Henry came into the kitchen, stooping slightly as he always did when he came through the doorway because of his height. Franny was helping Ida shell peas. There was an anxious look on his face. No, he didn't want a cup of coffee, he said. When Mrs. Stark stepped into the pantry, he turned quickly to Ida and Franny.

"You haven't seen Lady, have you? She never came in last night."

It was Franny who later found her. She was stretched out on her side under a little cedar tree in the overgrown pasture behind the barn. Her coat was matted and muddy, but she was alive. When Franny brought Henry to her, Lady tried to get up. She was stiff, and there was something wrong with her left front paw. Henry carried her up to the house in his arms.

Ida was scooping cottage cheese curds into a strainer lined with cheesecloth. She set it to drip over the pan of whey. "Mrs.

Stark's sorting linens upstairs. Bring the poor thing inside a moment."

Henry laid the old dog gently by the door. "She's hurt her foot. Now, why would she run off like that?" he said, looking helpless.

"Sometimes they get a wee bit daft when they're old. Franny, be a good girl and bring a basin of hot water and some rags." Ida poured some whey into a bowl and smiled when Lady lapped it and thumped her tail. "It's not leavin' this world you are yet, my girl." Ida knelt down beside Henry. "Now, let's see the hurt. Ah, look, there's something in it." Franny had brought the water, and now she fetched tweezers. In another few moments, Ida had pulled out a long thorn from a hawthorn tree. Lady whimpered, then relaxed and began licking her paw.

The three of them were kneeling on the floor together, cleaning up the old dog, Franny using her own hairbrush on the tangled fur, when Mrs. Stark came into the kitchen. Franny leapt to her feet.

"She was hungry and hurt, Mrs. Stark," she said.

Mrs. Stark did not speak for several moments. It was as if she were struggling for words potent enough for such an affront to the sterility of her kitchen. Then finally she spluttered, "Get that filthy creature out of here at once. Henry, believe me, Mrs. Morrow will know about this. Ida, I want the floor mopped with boiling water! And you, young miss," she said, with a grip like a claw on Franny's shoulder, "are going directly to your room."

———•———

It was July now. One day Franny and Meadowsweet watched, from the secret spot in the middle of the rhododendrons, as the iceman's truck pulled into the drive and stopped in front of the kitchen entryway. Veins bulged in the iceman's forehead as he carried the great dripping block clamped firmly in his iron tongs. Lady was lying in her spot at the bottom of the steps, waiting for Henry to finish his lunch. Burdened as he was, the iceman stepped carefully around the dog as he went up the steps. Mrs. Stark opened the door for him. In a minute he came out again. Mrs. Stark followed and stood a moment, fanning herself with a corner of her apron. She stared at Lady a moment, and her nostrils curled. Then she huffed down the concrete steps. Franny saw her heavy, black shoe snake out and kick the old dog. Franny found she was biting her lip as Lady yelped and stumbled away.

That day Franny wrote another letter to Papa:

Meadowsweet can't bear the Sea Hag. Grandmother doesn't even seem to notice how nasty she is. When Mrs. Stark was mean to Ida the other day, Meadowsweet stuck burdocks along the hem of her coat where they would get caught in her stockings.

When Mrs. Stark kicked Henry's dog, Meadowsweet was so mad she called her a fat old cow in front of Marigold, and Marigold was so insulted, she threatened to eat onion grass and sour her milk. Then Meadowsweet sneaked into Mrs. Stark's room and put a rose thorn in one of her shoes. . . .

Once again Franny felt her pen seeming to take on a life of its own. The words flowed almost in a torrent.

. . . Queen Iris was as mad as bees the other day because Meadowsweet's woolly bear caterpillar, Stripesy, chewed up her new pink lupine slippers. "It's enough to send one into strong hysterics," Iris said to Tamarack, "and Isadora Toad charged me seven columbine seeds for them, which was nothing short of highway robbery."

"There, there, dearest," said Tamarack. "We certainly are not wanting for seeds. You shall have a new pair."

"That's not the point," pouted Iris. "They were from near the tip of the stalk where you find the best-fitting ones, and I had to fly up there and get them myself. Isadora can no more hop that high than she can fly. I have half a mind to tell her that with her figure, she has no business running a slipper shop." She looked at the tattered slippers and began to sniffle.

"Stripesy chewed them because they smell like

pepper, Mama," said Meadowsweet, holding Stripesy protectively. "You know how much she loves pepper. Maybe you should buy trefoil slippers next time."

From then on, night after night when she was supposed to be asleep, Franny wrote letters to Papa. She told about Meadowsweet's close call with the barn owl when she was trying to visit the swallow and pigeon babies. She told about the tricks she played on Mrs. Stark, how Tamarack saved Isadora Toad's even fatter sister from the black snake in the garden, and she told about the tiger lily gown Iris wore to her lawn party on the billiard table in the cellar. She wrote letters until only a few sheets were left in the box Mama had given her. She carefully addressed and stamped each one and left it in the basket outside the front door for the postman to take to Papa.

———◆———

IDA PROTECTED FRANNY FROM MRS. STARK, AND IN TURN, Franny protected Ida. Franny ran to wipe up her own spills, and slipped into the kitchen to help when she could. Knowing that Ida would let herself be used, Franny said she liked to help wash dishes or peel potatoes. Her hands were healed now, but there were pink, shiny scars left. She tended to hide them still, especially when Mrs. Stark's black *look* raked her up and down.

"Ida," Mrs. Stark said one morning, "there are mouse droppings in this souffle dish. I want a trap set on that top shelf."

"I'm afraid I'll be snappin' me own fingers, reachin' things down from up there, Mrs. Stark. There's a lovely litter of kittens down in the barn. Franny discovered them. One's a calico. They're wonderful mousers, you know. I could have Mr. B bring her up when she's old enough."

"You can just nip that idea in the bud, miss. If there's one thing I cannot abide, it's the insinuating ways of a cat. They're Satan's own helpmates, if you ask me, licking the butter when your back's turned and sneaking onto beds and trying to smother infants. There are far too many cats in that barn. I asked Mr. B to drown any kittens he found this summer. If he hasn't done it, I'll do it myself. It won't be the first time. And any ninny who can't remember where she's put a mousetrap deserves what she gets."

Franny shuddered and slipped away to the barn as soon as she had a chance. "You won't drown the kittens, will you, Mr. B?" she blurted out.

Mr. B chuckled and rubbed his chin. "As long as Mrs. Stark doesn't know about 'em, they're safe enough. She's got it in for cats, does that woman."

"She does know about them."

"Well, then, don't you worry. I'll carry them down to the house and the wife'll find some neighbors to take them when they're old enough. That's what she generally does."

———•———

THAT EVENING GRANDMOTHER HAD A HEADACHE AND went to bed early. Franny wasn't sorry. She was sure that

Grandmother played cards and checkers with her in the evening only to be polite. Neither of them tried very hard to win, and so the games were dull.

As soon as Grandmother had gone upstairs, Franny tiptoed to the kitchen looking for Ida. She wasn't there, but Franny found her out on the screened porch. It was a night of fireflies and crickets in the damp grass. The porch was a nice place. There were prints on the wall on each side of the French doors—spring, summer, fall, and winter birds. The scent of Grandmother's roses drifted in from the garden. There were wicker chairs and a table, and a convenient ledge all around for a dish of crackers or a cup of tea.

There was no electric light on the porch. Ida looked almost peaceful with her dark hair gleaming in the light of the coal oil lamp. The pillowcase she meant to be mending lay untouched in her lap. She looked up and smiled when Franny pulled up one of the wicker chairs and sat down. They sat in friendly silence for perhaps twenty minutes before Mrs. Stark appeared.

"It is high time little ladies were in bed," she growled with a look that allowed no argument. Reluctantly, Franny said good night to Ida and went upstairs.

It was in the morning as Franny ate her breakfast alone— Grandmother had gone to her lecture—that Ida slipped into the dining room to tell her.

"I saw them, Franny."

"What, Ida?"

"Little folk. Last night on the screened porch. Not the leprechaun, but 'twas fairy folk my own two eyes saw—not this big," and she held her hands about six inches apart. "The most shimmerin', lovely green. I thought sure they didna see me in the gloom, but then it came to me that p'rhaps they'd come special to me."

Franny smiled eagerly. "I think they might be garden fairies. I knew they'd come. But why do you think they came to see you, Ida?"

"To tell me to put my cares away and open me eyes. To tell me that this America has a bit of magic too. I tell you I was that amazed. I blessed the Holy Virgin. . . . 'Tis the little people, a world of spirits awatchin', makin' mischief mayhap, but sometimes aidin' a soul. Oh, Franny, I thought America was as dead as me heart."

AFTER BREAKFAST, FRANNY FOUND MEADOWSWEET SITTING with Stripesy beside the pool under the big pine tree. She was fishing with a long hair from Bobby's mane.

"Meadowsweet, there are no fish in there," said Franny.

"I know, I'm just practicing for someday when I'll live by a *real* pond." Meadowsweet kicked her heels in the pine needles as if she were in a mood.

"Ida saw some of the garden fairies last night."

"I see them all the time, Franny, but they're really stuck-up. They never talk to me."

"Meadowsweet, shame on you," Iris broke in. She had come to fill a shell basin with water. "You're not giving them a chance. I've found that people who seem unfriendly are often merely shy."

"Why don't you and I go meet them tonight?" asked Franny.

Meadowsweet looked at her mama and then down at her feet.

"I'm afraid she can't, Franny," Iris said. "Meadowsweet was very naughty this morning. Tell Franny what you did, young lady."

Meadowsweet looked miserable. She rolled her eyes and muttered, "I put a baby centipede on Mrs. Stark's breakfast toast."

Franny clapped her hand over her mouth for a moment to keep from laughing. "Oh, Meadowsweet, you didn't!"

"Yes, she did, Franny," said Iris severely, "and it was very unkind to the poor little thing. Its mother had to clean crab apple jelly off all those feet, not to mention the danger to both of them."

"Oh, Mama, no one has sharper eyes than Mrs. Stark. She'd never have bitten into it, and you know very well she can't see me anyway."

"But she could still crush you accidentally. You are to stay strictly away from her."

That night Franny crept downstairs alone, after Grandmother and Mrs. Stark were in bed, to watch for the garden fairies with Ida. The moon washed the garden in silver, and the soft air of the summer night lifted the leaves of the shrubbery, casting flickering shadows. Ida lighted the lamp. She sat pensively, her fingers pressed against her temples.

"What's wrong?" asked Franny.

Ida smiled faintly and shook her head. "I was just thinking that if I could climb Croagh Patrick with the pilgrims next Eastertime and lay a little stone from me father's farm on Saint Patrick's cairn at the peak, God might forgive me sins. . . ."

"What sins, Ida?"

But Ida shook her head. "I'll not trouble a young heart," she murmured.

They watched the big gray spider in the eaves over the screen door. Most of the time she didn't move, but when a mosquito blundered into her net, she dropped quickly to wrap it up. Franny thought of Tamarack's great battle with the orb weaver spider. Fireflies blinked on and off on the lawn, and Franny could see down in the pasture beside the barn millions of their little flashing lights.

" 'Tis said the wee folk tame them and carry them for lanterns," breathed Ida. Franny nodded to herself. She felt alive all over, every pore, every nerve and tiny hair of her body feeling the night. The moon glowed. It seemed to pour liquid magic into the little world of Grandmother's garden.

Then it was there—a fluttering of wings, like Mama's gauze scarf, near the mulberry tree. It was green in the moonlight, pale fairy green. Franny felt as if Papa were sitting there beside her. She could almost feel the warmth of his arm around her shoulder.

The fairy danced closer and paused a moment on the screen. Ida made a sound in her throat, in fear or joy, Franny couldn't tell. The green wings tapered gracefully into tails. They had strange, golden eyelike markings on them, exactly like the markings on Tamarack's and Iris's wings. Franny could even see tiny ferny antennae just like theirs. She wanted to get up and move closer, to talk to it, but garden fairies were so shy. She didn't want to frighten it away.

A minute passed, or maybe forever, but suddenly the fairy was gone. Franny saw that Ida was breathing quickly and trembling. She laughed softly, fearful of awakening Mrs. Stark.

"You see!" said Ida triumphantly. "They will not show themselves to just anyone. It is that we believe. They've chosen us."

Franny looked at Ida and the words came slowly. She knew the time was right. "There are other fairies here, Ida. There's King Tamarack, Queen Iris, and Princess Meadowsweet. My papa believed in them. He used to tell me their stories. . . . He wrote them all out on paper too. Mama didn't like the stories. When Papa . . . when Papa went away, she burned them up." Franny twisted her fingers in her lap. "That's how I burnt my hands. I tried to save the stories." She stopped suddenly, struggling for words. Her eyes grew very bright in the lamplight. "My mama was wrong, Ida. Papa would never lie to me. There *are* real fairies."

Chapter Thirteen ⤳

IDA WAS CHANGED. THERE WAS A LIGHT NOW IN HER EYES. To Franny it was as plain as a sunrise. When Henry came in with a fine mess of trout after his day off, it was as if Ida suddenly saw him for the first time. She smiled at him and he went away speechless with embarrassment.

She made oatmeal cookies that filled the kitchen with the scent of cinnamon and allspice. Franny ate three of them with a big glass of milk before Mrs. Stark removed the platter. "They are much too rich for a child's digestion," she croaked in her seagull voice. Franny was fairly sure that she ate the rest of the cookies herself, probably washed down with salt water.

Later, as Ida was dusting the shelf on the stair landing, Franny heard a sound, breathy and sweet, almost as if the warblers had come back to life. It took her a moment to realize Ida was singing.

But Mrs. Stark treated Ida more grimly than ever. "If you think you can manage it, I'd like to see that upper bath clean this time," and, when Mr. B brought in a peck basket of new potatoes, "Ida'll wash them up. She doesn't mind a little dirt." Or it was, "I'll not be asked to cook in a pan as carelessly scoured as this. It might do in the shanty full of brats you were brought up in, but it won't do in this house." There was no mistaking the sneering tone. Ida took back the offending pan meekly, but Franny seethed. Later she tugged all the antimacassars in the parlor out of place, yanked back the drapes, and emptied the bowl of lump sugar into her pinafore pocket for Bobby Burns.

Henry seemed to be around the kitchen more and more. One night, when Grandmother had again gone to bed early and Franny was sitting with Ida on the porch, he appeared by the steps with Lady at his heels, turning a dog brush awkwardly in his hands.

"I bought this so's you could brush Lady proper, like you do Bobby Burns," he said to Franny.

"Best do it outside, Franny," cautioned Ida.

They went out and sat on the steps in the twilight. Lady leaned into the brushing with a happy sigh. Ida brought Franny a cup of tea and sat on the top step.

Henry couldn't seem to think of anything to say, so Ida thought of something.

"Where did you learn about automobiles?" she asked him.

He seemed embarrassed. "Oh, I don't know half what there is to know. I just picked up bits here and there working around my dad's shop down in Haverhill, and I read journals. But that Cadillac, now, she's a dandy. Got an electric starter, you know. Best idea yet. Friend of mine broke his wrist cranking the starter on a Ford." There was a sort of reverence in Henry's voice when he spoke about Grandmother's car.

"But what about horses? Don't you care about them? What if nobody ever wants horses anymore now that they have automobiles?" Franny worried.

"Sure I like horses, kid. Even our old pony, Pal, that me and Jim rode to school. Every spring he got rambunctious and bucked us off, but we still liked him fine."

"Horses were given to us for special friends, just like dogs," said Ida softly. "There'll always be folk as will keep a horse, even if it's just to ride for the pleasure of it."

Then Franny told them about how she sometimes slipped onto Bobby Burns's back, and how she would dream with her arms around his neck while he cropped the short grass of his pasture.

"Now, you must be careful, he's not a trained riding horse, I hear," warned Ida. "We had a pony too, when I was little. Well, she really belonged to the farmer next door. He said if we could catch her, we could ride her. We caught her all right, but she was as slippery and flighty as a will-o'-the-wisp. When she ran she was lovely and dainty footed, but many's the time she'd take a notion to dance on her hind legs and toss us in the grass. Next time you're thinkin' of ridin' Bobby, why don't you let me lead you—if Mrs. Stark will let me slip away for a bit."

Franny saw that Henry's eyes were on Ida as she talked. There was something very deep in them.

Ida stroked Lady's head. "Mr. Black, the innkeeper in our village, had a fine hunting dog just like your Lady. Is she a good bird dog?"

"Used to bring me pa'tridges I'd not even shot sometimes. She can still smell 'em, but she gets awful stiff now."

Ida looked up at the first stars coming out and began to hum. After a few moments, Henry looked at her strangely and said, as if mesmerized, *"Turn ye to me . . ."*

"You know that tune?" Ida's eyes widened.

Henry unfolded himself from the bottom step where he had been sitting beside Franny. "I'll be right back." When he returned, he held a pennywhistle in his hands. "My granddad taught me a lot of old tunes when I was a boy. He used to play the fiddle. We had dances." He put the whistle to his lips and began to play a melody that seemed to lift and fall like ocean waves while Ida sang about stars and seabirds calling and a lonely heart.

Some of the words were incomprehensible to Franny: *"Ho ro Mhairi dhu,* turn ye to me . . . it's Gaelic, a Scottish song, really, and very old," Ida explained. "It was a favorite of me mother's." Then a lilting reel spilled into the air, as if out of nowhere. Ida's foot began to tap. Henry played another, in a minor key this time, but the notes danced so wildly that Franny's foot began to tap too. As the pennywhistle leapt into yet another melody, Ida jumped to her feet, clasping Franny's hands and pulling her up with her.

"Well, now, we'll not insult the piper!" She hitched up her

skirt and put her hands on her hips. Her feet began to move so quickly that they seemed to have a life of their own. Franny moved awkwardly at first, trying to copy the way Ida's feet went up and down and around and around. She began to feel dizzy. But then the music seemed to creep inside her and suddenly her feet knew what to do. Henry grinned and the pennywhistle played. Ida whirled, eyes flashing in the light from the lamp. Franny panted and giggled.

"Look at the child now, will you," Ida called to Henry. "I thought we'd never see her laugh."

Suddenly Mrs. Stark loomed large and black in the doorway from the dining room. "That will be enough of that racket," she said in a voice like creaking ice. "That child should have been in bed an hour ago."

THE NEXT MORNING WHEN FRANNY SAW HENRY IN THE kitchen, he winked at her. "You're a good dancer, kid," he whispered. Franny beamed and glanced over to where Ida was washing dishes at the big soapstone sink. She gave them both a secret smile.

"Ida, you'd better be getting at the ironing," Mrs. Stark croaked as she sailed into the kitchen from the dining room. Ida obediently went into the back room to fetch the ironing board, iron, and the basket of sprinkled and tightly rolled clothes from yesterday's washing. Mrs. Stark disappeared into the dining room where Grandmother was lingering over a cup of coffee, and came back a few moments later, announcing, "Mrs. Morrow would like lemonade for the pastor's visit this afternoon. I'll need the Sandwich glass pitcher." But Ida was still in the back room. With a snort of disgust, Mrs. Stark reached for the pitcher herself. There was a loud snap, and a strangled cry. Mrs. Stark whirled around, clutching the tips of her fingers, and glared like a snake at Henry and Franny. A livid spot of color, the first Franny had ever seen, appeared on each gray cheek.

<hr />

ON MRS. STARK'S NEXT DAY OFF FRANNY WAS HEADED FOR the attic stairs almost before the car was out of the driveway with Henry taking the housekeeper to town. She started to turn toward the shelves of flat boxes when she spied a big, old traveling trunk in a corner. The fastenings were stiff, but after a bit she pried them open and lifted the lid. What she saw made her gasp so loudly that it brought Tamarack, Iris, and Meadowsweet hurrying to her side. Tamarack and Meadowsweet scurried to the top of a box, but Iris forgot herself. She unfolded her wings, and in a blur of green and gold, they lifted her to hover by Franny's shoulder.

There, on a folded, white woolen blanket, scattered with mothballs, lay a slate-blue bird with a snowy ruff and belly, glass eyes bright, its beak gleaming like a dagger. It looked ready to unfold its wings and hurl itself through the air with that chattering call that Papa said was like pebbles in a tin can.

"The kingfisher," Tamarack groaned. Meadowsweet hid her face on his shoulder.

"Are you sure?" asked Iris, alighting next to him. "Mightn't it be another bird?"

"No," said Tamarack. "That's the scar from the wound he took during the battle with the hornpout, and look here: one of the crown feathers and some from this wing are missing. Besides, I'd know my old friend anywhere."

There didn't seem to be anything to do then, except close the lid of the trunk softly.

———•———

A few minutes later, heart pounding, Franny tapped on Grandmother's study door. "Come in," her grandmother called in a voice that sounded as though she wasn't very interested in having a visitor just then. Franny thought about tiptoeing away, but Meadowsweet was in the basket saying, "Please, Franny, you have to do it." So she went in.

"I need to ask you something." Her voice sounded harsh in the quiet room. Grandmother glanced up from the large volume that lay on the table before her. She looked at Franny over her spectacles. Franny paused. The room was a confusion of half-open drawers and shelves, dusty books, jars and bottles, rolls of drawing paper, brushes and pencils.

"Yes, Franny?"

Franny bit her lip and took a breath to steady herself.

"Grandmother, if you love birds so much, why do you kill them?"

Grandmother's mouth opened and then closed and she was silent a moment. "I see what you mean," she said finally to Franny. "It doesn't seem right, I suppose. At the time, it seemed like the only way to really study them, and to answer certain questions. I used to catch them in nets and chloroform them. It must sound cruel to you. And I could never capture the way they look in life, in my models, no matter how delicately I treated the skins and mounted them. Actually, Franny, I don't kill them anymore. I guess, after a time, it didn't seem right to me either. I'm sorry for it. Friends bring me birds that they find—if they are in good condition. See, here's a cardinal that hit a window at the parsonage. Did you ever see such color?"

In spite of herself, Franny gazed at the gorgeous red and black bird that lay in the drawer Grandmother had pulled open. "Best not touch it, Franny," Grandmother cautioned. "I have to treat them with arsenic to preserve them. Next winter, when I've more time, I'll mount this one. He's a beauty. We called them redbirds in Tennessee. How I loved to hear them whistling in the tree outside my window when I was a girl. They used to be rare in the North, but now that people are putting seed out for wild birds, you sometimes see one."

"Grandmother," Franny said slowly, "there's a kingfisher in a trunk in the attic. What happened to him?"

Grandmother looked puzzled. Then she gave a little laugh.

119

"Oh, that. Your father found him lying on the beach one time when he was fishing at Larch Pond. He'd lost a few feathers, but he was quite fresh. I wasn't really satisfied with the way he turned out. I decided it would have been more exciting to mount him with his wings spread and a fish in his beak, and then there were the missing feathers. I suppose I'm a bit of a perfectionist. It was odd, though. Arthur said there was a dead hornpout nearby with a feather in its mouth, as if the two had been fighting—but that seems impossible, of course."

"What did Papa do with the feathers?"

"If I remember correctly, he gave them to Henry for tying flies for trout fishing. He's quite good at it."

———

AT DINNER, IDA ASKED GRANDMOTHER SHYLY IF IT WOULD be all right if she took the same day off as Henry. Grandmother said yes. Mrs. Stark was indignant. "I think you'll be sorry, Mrs. Morrow. That one's not to be trusted," she said darkly after Ida had gone back to the kitchen.

"Why, Judith, I think it's lovely that the two want to go out together. Henry's not so very much older than Ida, and he's been so lonely since his Sarah died. Besides, they asked particularly if they might take Franny with them. I'm sure it will do the child good."

Franny bristled somewhat at being talked about as if she weren't there, but she was glad that Grandmother gave permission. Eagerly she hurried out to the kitchen herself, as soon as the meal was over. Henry looked up from where he was finishing his supper at the kitchen table. "So it's to be an expedition," he said with a smile.

"Yes, and Grandmother says I can go too."

"Well, then, what would you ladies like to do?"

Ida was washing up at the sink, her cheeks flushed. Before she could answer, Franny said, "We could go fishing!" She took a quick breath, hoping she wasn't being rude.

"Yes, that would be lovely," agreed Ida. "We could take the little boat out on the pond."

"No . . ." Franny stammered, looking anxiously from one to the other. "I meant trout fishing along the brook with flies. . . ."

"I've got only one fly rod . . ." Henry began to say, but Franny interrupted him.

"We could take turns. You could give us lessons. And it's so hot, it would be cooler in the woods than out on the pond."

"Aye, that it would," said Ida, wiping her face with the corner of her apron. "I've a longin' to jump right in a cold brook this minute."

And so they went. Franny brought her basket so Meadowsweet could go too. Iris didn't care for fishing, and Tamarack had to repair wind damage in the castle.

"Careful," he had warned Meadowsweet. "Remember that feather's tied to a hook now. You'll have to be very clever to get it without getting stabbed."

Ida packed a lunch. The three of them walked down the farm road, past a little abandoned sawmill, into a shady woods of pine and hemlock. They came to an old stone bridge made of two huge granite slabs laid side by side. Upstream, a small waterfall rushed between hemlock roots and over a boulder into a swirling pool of bubbles.

Franny shivered as they crossed the bridge to get to the path that followed the brook. Moss clung, dripping from the two huge rocks, and the air was chilly and damp. The brook disappeared into a dark place underneath the stones and came out again on the other side. There was a gap in between the boulders wide enough to catch your foot if you weren't careful. She could see down into the blackness between them, and for just a moment, she thought she saw something glisten and disappear, something like an eye or a tooth. It certainly did look like a good place for a troll. She had to remind herself that trolls couldn't bear daylight.

Henry motioned for Ida and Franny to stay where they were on the bank. To Franny's disappointment, he put a worm on a hook and dropped it right into the middle of the tumbling water below the waterfall. For a second Franny saw the worm being tossed about. Then suddenly it was gone and Henry's rod tip began to twitch. In another moment a brook trout came wriggling out of the water on the end of his line. Henry held it for Franny to see. Its sides were flecked with brilliant speckles; its bottom fins were bright orange lined with white.

He slipped the fish into his creel and let Ida and Franny try. Ida caught one, but twice Franny felt the line tugging only to have the trout flip back into the foaming water as soon as she tried to pull it up. After the second time, Franny knelt down, trying to see where the fish had disappeared. From the basket, Meadowsweet whispered something in her ear. Franny nodded.

"Maybe they don't like worms today, Henry," said Franny. "Maybe they'd rather go after flies."

"Nah, there are too many branches here to cast properly. We'll try flies farther up." Franny and Ida hitched up their skirts and followed Henry along the mossy side of the brook. Sometimes they hopped from stone to stone right in the brook. Soon each of them had at least one wet foot. Franny's hem was soaked, but her cheeks were pink with excitement. The water was liquid ice.

Franny tried fishing again. "You have to give it a little tug to set the hook," said Henry. Even when she focused all her attention on the spot where the line vanished into the water, Franny was surprised by the next tug. But this time she managed to tug back. Then at last, squealing, she pounced on the slippery little fish that flopped about in the ferns.

They walked up to a beaver pond and Henry took out a small tin box from his pocket and opened it. Franny's heart beat quickly. It was full of trout flies.

"Oh, let me see them!" exclaimed Ida. "Why, they're lovely. Where did you get such things?"

"Made 'em myself," Henry muttered awkwardly.

Franny looked too. The flies were all colors, red, brown, golden—and one had a *slate-blue feather,* like a tail, tied with a tuft of some sort of white fur. As Franny gazed at it, the kingfisher's feather seemed to catch an air current and move as if it wanted to float away on its own. It gleamed like water and sky as it twisted in the sunlight. Ida reached out and stroked the tiny feather. "It's lovely," she murmured.

Before Franny could open her mouth or think what to say, Henry took out the fly and hooked it onto the band of Ida's little felt hat, saying, "Never caught a darn thing with it anyway." Franny could feel Meadowsweet kicking with frustration against the sides of the basket.

Henry cleaned the fish they caught on a stone beside the brook, but when they returned home and emptied the creel into the kitchen sink to give the trout a final rinse, Franny stared at them sadly. The colors had faded. The fish were gray and blotchy where they'd lain together. The brilliant flecks of color on their sides were gone. She turned to say something to Ida, but Ida was just going up the stairs, taking off her hat as she went, to put it away.

At bedtime, Franny and Meadowsweet held a council. "What do we do now?" Franny asked. "Henry gave it to Ida— she thinks it's hers now. I don't see how we can ever get it."

"Franny," said Meadowsweet, "that was supposed to be my feather. I need it to fly. There has to be a way! If you can go snooping in Mrs. Stark's room, you can certainly sneak into Ida's room and snitch that fly off her hat."

"But this is different. Ida's my friend."

Meadowsweet crossed her arms and glared at Franny. "Who's your better friend, me or Ida?"

"Meadowsweet, you know you're my best friend in the whole world. It's just that I really like Ida a lot." She stopped. "Meadowsweet? Are you jealous?"

Meadowsweet ignored the question. "Franny, she'd probably just think she lost it somewhere."

"Oh, but Meadowsweet, Henry gave it to her. It would be wrong for me to take it."

"Well, I think it would be a whole lot more wrong if I never got to fly."

Chapter Fourteen ⌒

WITH HER HEART IN HER MOUTH, FRANNY WATCHED IDA for the right moment. She thought it had come one morning when Ida left to walk to the post office to mail a small package home to her mother in Ireland. She'd shown Franny the delicate lace collar as she was working on it. "There, now, me mother can wear this and know I'm not forgettin' all she taught me. And, I'm sendin' twenty dollars," she added, rolling the number on her tongue proudly, "so Eileen and the boys can buy a few things and remember their big sister."

As she was going out the door, she put a hand to her hair. "Well, now, I've forgotten me hat and the postmistress will think me a fine thing." Then she smiled at Franny. "Ah, but it's such a lovely day, the sun will feel good. Do ye want to walk with me, Franny?"

"No. I mean, yes, but I guess I should work some on my sampler."

Ida laughed. "Now you are an odd one. See you in a bit then."

Mrs. Stark was in the kitchen making a new supply of dry and tasteless tea cakes. With her heart beating loudly in her ears, Franny tiptoed down the upstairs hallway past Mrs. Stark's bedroom door to Ida's room. Her hand was on the doorknob when she heard Grandmother's voice. It was coming from the bottom of the stairs.

"Are you up there, Franny?"

As quietly as she could, Franny went back to the upstairs landing. "Yes, Grandmother?"

"Franny, I've left my spectacles on my dressing table. Could I trouble you to fetch them?" Before Franny could get up the nerve to try again, Ida was back from the post office.

THE NEXT TIME IDA AND HENRY HAD THE DAY OFF, THEY decided to go fishing at Larch Pond. Meadowsweet begged her parents to let her go along too.

"Oh, 'Sweet, I don't think so."

"Why not, Mama?" asked Meadowsweet.

"You know perfectly well why not," her mother replied.

"Just to go in the boat, Mama, and picnic. I promise I won't swim."

Iris frowned and glanced at Tamarack.

"I don't see what harm it would do, love," he said. "Even if she did swim, I'm sure she'd come to no harm, but since she's promised not to, I think a boating expedition would be good fun. We could all go. I'd really like to see the old place again, myself. Besides, it might be a chance to recover the feather." And so it was settled.

This must be where the battle with the hornpout took place, thought Franny as she stepped into the stern of the old rowboat and sat down next to Ida. It's exactly the way Papa described it. She placed the basket safely beside her and looked around at the small, sandy beach, the little swamp thick with cattails, and the single huge larch tree that grew by itself, away from the other trees, near the shore. A small painted turtle slid off a lily pad, making the white blossom floating beside it bob in the water. So much had happened here. Franny opened the lid of the basket so that Tamarack and his family could enjoy the trip too.

In spite of herself, Iris loved boating. She had brought a nasturtium leaf parasol to keep off the sun, and sat, daydreaming, with her eyes half closed. Tamarack was busy pointing out the sights to Meadowsweet. As the boat slid through the water, past the larch tree, Franny could see the hollows under its roots where it had grown over a log, long since melted back into the ground. What a wonderful house it must have been! She thought she could make out a broken-down porch, and there were definitely stone steps leading up to the old front entryway. Tamarack pointed to a small hollow partway up the trunk. "That was my room, and then later your nursery," he said to Meadowsweet, "and between those boulders on the shore is where we kept our boat."

Iris sighed. "Yes, those were good years," she admitted, "until Meadowsweet got completely out of control in the water. I thought I'd have a breakdown! You can't imagine how glad I was to move to Cambridge."

Tamarack smiled. "Oh, it was a grand old place. When I was a boy, it used to ring with many a full moon gathering."

It was a dreamy, lazy day. Even the fish seemed too lazy to bite, but no one really minded. After a bit, Tamarack closed his eyes and napped, giving an occasional snore. Franny hummed or coughed and shuffled her feet to cover it up. But Meadowsweet was restless. She couldn't take her eyes off the fly in Ida's hatband.

They ate sandwiches in the boat. Then later, as the sun was going down, hot and red, behind the pines, Franny felt a terrific pull on her line. "Easy, easy," cautioned Henry as she yanked back, but the fish didn't shake itself free. It circled, deep in the water, while Franny struggled to reel it in. When it came up out of the water at last, she gave a little scream. It was a hornpout, greenish black with a yellow belly, tossing its whiskered head from side to side and glaring at her with angry eyes as it opened and closed its big mouth. She was glad when Henry took it off the hook for her. He held it expertly, so the barbs wouldn't puncture his fingers, as he worked the hook loose.

"Stepped on one of these when I was a kid. Got so infected I hobbled around on one foot most of the summer," he said. "Some say they're poison, but they ain't. 'S just pond slime. Mighty good eating once they're skinned out, though."

As they were rowing back to shore, gliding into the shadows of some overhanging trees, Meadowsweet saw her chance. Ida took off her hat a moment and set it on the seat beside her while she fixed her hair. Meadowsweet slipped out of the basket and crept along the floorboards toward Ida's seat, her eyes fixed on the kingfisher's feather. Then suddenly, there was a rustle in the drooping branch of a hemlock, followed by a squeak. Franny glimpsed a little bundle of gray fur scrambling desperately, then suddenly plunging into the water a few yards away from the boat.

"A baby squirrel!" she cried as it disappeared beneath the surface. She saw it come up as Henry rowed toward it, then go under again. Meadowsweet forgot the hat and the trout fly with the kingfisher's feather in it. She leapt to the gunwale of the rowboat.

"Meadowsweet, NO!" screamed Iris. But her daughter paid no attention to her and dove over the side.

They stared into the water. It was deep here, even so close to the shore, and looked almost black in the fading daylight. "If only the poor little mite would come up again," said Ida sadly. But Franny was thinking of fish and water snakes. What if one should think Meadowsweet was some sort of darting silver minnow? She shuddered.

Tamarack held Iris tightly. "Hush, love, it's her element," he murmured. "Some time she must go to it."

The seconds seemed to drag on. Then suddenly, there was a motion on the surface and a little whiskered nose and huge, frightened eyes emerged. Franny could see that Meadowsweet had her arms around the squirrel, holding it up. For just the flicker of an instant, she thought she saw something else, a tiny face, like Meadowsweet's, only with golden hair. Then it vanished again. Henry reached out the blade of his oar and the little sodden creature scrambled onto it. He swung it over toward Franny.

She held out her skirt and took the tiny squirrel. Just then she heard a rattling cry, and looked up to see a slate-blue bird swoop low over the water of the cove to perch in the larch tree. Moments later Meadowsweet had scrambled into her lap too, helping to dry the squirrel off with Franny's handkerchief. Franny had never seen a squirrel like this one. Its eyes were enormous. Its tail seemed flattened underneath, and there were loose folds of skin along its sides.

"It's a flying squirrel," said Henry. "They used to spook me, skimming over my head when I had to make a late-night run to the backhouse when I was a boy. We used to call them fairy diddles—kinda suits 'em—you might mistake 'em for a fairy."

Ida stroked the damp fur with a gentle finger. "It's so tiny, can it live, do ye think?" Franny looked anxiously at Henry.

"It's old enough to have its eyes open; that's good. They don't get as big as other squirrels anyway. Your grandma'll know what to do with it."

———————

Grandmother Morrow's eyes lighted up as if they'd brought her a birthday cake. Franny tried to imagine Nana

DiCrista cradling a baby squirrel in her hand, feeding it warm milk from an eyedropper, and laughing when it sneezed a little milky sneeze onto the waist of her dress. She shook her head. It was an impossible picture, but for Grandmother Morrow, it seemed perfectly natural.

"Is it not young for this late in the summer?" asked Ida.

Grandmother shook her head. "Squirrels often have a second litter," she said.

After a moment's struggle, the squirrel took the dropper in his two paws and nursed greedily. "We'll get some goat's milk from Mrs. Lawson in the morning—he'll do better on that. I think it's a little boy, Franny. What would you like to name him?"

Franny felt a tiny flicker of warmth at the sudden ease in Grandmother's manner. "I'll call him Diddle," she said shyly.

Henry fixed a wooden crate with a screened cover and Grandmother found an old woolen hat. Diddle's fur was dry and fluffy now. It was shorter and denser than any fur Franny had ever touched. He seemed to like the feeling of Franny's finger stroking him. Franny thought maybe it reminded him of his mother, licking. He didn't seem to have suffered too much from his dunking. As soon as he finished his supper, they showed him the hat and he burrowed into it and fell asleep. Ida brought a hot water bottle and they snuggled it next to the hat.

"We'll have to feed him during the night," said Grandmother.

Franny was allowed to keep Diddle's box in her room. "When he gets bigger, we'll move him to the screened porch," said Grandmother. "Mrs. Stark will have a fit. I've finally gotten her to stop sweeping down the phoebe's nests from under the eaves. Now she'll have to put up with a squirrel in the house. I suppose she'll be livid when I ask her to take up the mousetraps. It's been a few years since your father and uncles brought wild things in."

Sometimes Franny woke in the night to see Grandmother warming Diddle's little cup of milk over a candle flame and feeding him in the flickering circle of light, but often it was Meadowsweet who woke her with a tug on the earlobe, and the two of them fed him themselves.

Meadowsweet had fallen completely in love with the little creature she had rescued. For the moment all thoughts of the kingfisher's feather were forgotten. She even slept beside him to keep him warm, though he was nearly as big as she was. Stripesy was jealous until she was allowed to sleep in the hat as well. Meadowsweet even stayed home to help take care of Diddle when, the following Saturday, Franny went to the ocean with Henry and Ida. She was a very businesslike babysitter, with her sleeves rolled up, one of Iris's aprons tied around her waist, and a slippery-elm twig in her pocket for a teether. "Just you go now, and don't worry, Franny," she said, stroking her enormous baby's head. She rubbed noses with him and he stared at her with his big, bright eyes. "Diddle and I will have lots of fun together, won't we?"

So Franny went to the beach with Ida and Henry by herself. When they arrived, Cape Ann, to the south of them, was hidden in fog, but by ten o'clock, the hot sun of early August had burned it off and they could see the great summer houses along the rocky coast. They bathed in the cold, salty ocean water, glad for their woolen suits, and walked far down the beach. Henry fished in the surf. Ida sat nearby watching while Franny gathered shells and seaweed and, just for fun, made a little house in the sand. "But Iris wouldn't like a sand house," she told Ida. "It would dry up or get washed away by the waves, and she would be terrified of the seagulls."

"Tell me more about your fairies, Franny," Ida said softly.

"Tamarack is like Papa. He knows everything about the woods and loves to joke. Iris is sort of like Mama. You know, always fussing about keeping your clothes clean, and she knows how to sew really well. And Meadowsweet is like me, sort of, but wilder. She gets into trouble a lot. I'm not pretty like her though."

Ida raised an eyebrow. "Now, whatever put that foolishness into your head? The swan in the story did not start out elegant and graceful, you know. Someday Miss Frances Morrow will turn a few heads, I'm thinkin'."

Franny cringed. "Oh, Ida, I just hate my name. Mama did it. Papa always said he wanted to name me Emerald, or Titania, but Mama wouldn't hear of it. Frances is so . . . so fusty. I wish I could have at least been named something pretty."

Ida laughed. Then she said earnestly, "I think it's lovely. The saint of that name could talk to the animals."

———•———

THE NEXT WEEK, HENRY AND IDA HELPED FRANNY scramble onto Bobby Burns's back while Mr. B shook his head and chuckled. Then they led her down the farm road as far as the brook and back. Bobby lifted his feet and cocked his ears. Coming back toward the barn, Franny saw Grandmother standing on her garden steps watching them. She couldn't make out Grandmother's face well enough to see her expression. The old woman watched them for a few moments, then turned and went back to her garden.

"He's a happier horse, he is these days, eh Bobby-boy?" said Mr. B, coming out of his toolshed to stroke the old horse's neck.

They picked blueberries and Ida made pies. When Henry sat down at the kitchen table to a thick slice, still warm from the oven, with whipped cream melting on it, Franny thought the look on Ida's face was as satisfied as if she were eating it herself.

One evening, when Franny and Meadowsweet were coming into the kitchen to get milk for Diddle, they almost bumped into Henry and Ida, just returned from a walk. Ida's hat had fallen to the floor, and she was stooping to pick it up. Her cheeks were flushed. Franny could tell she had been laughing.

" 'Night, Miss Franny, Ida . . ." said Henry a bit sheepishly. The two exchanged a look, and Henry closed the door behind himself.

"How's the wee nutkin?" asked Ida.

"He's starting to climb all over the place," Franny answered. "Yesterday afternoon I found him on top of the owl's head in the upstairs hall, and this morning I found him eating a soda cracker. I think he must have stolen it from the pantry. He's starting to like nuts and dog biscuits better than his milk."

Ida smiled. "That's fine now, Franny. Well, we'd both best get to bed," she added.

"I should say so," Mrs. Stark said moodily as she entered the kitchen in her nightdress and slippers. She stalked over to the stove, lifted a lid, and stirred up the coals under the teakettle. Ida went upstairs. Franny filled a little tin cup with goat's milk from the bottle in the icebox and set it on a corner of the stove to warm.

"If that creature comes anywhere near my bedroom, I'll set a rat trap," Mrs. Stark muttered. She was just turning from the cupboard with a mug in her hand.

Franny could feel Meadowsweet in her pocket quivering with rage. She felt the water sprite start climbing out of the pocket. Then she heard her shrill whisper, "Franny, *look*!" In the same instant, all three pairs of eyes fell on an object in the middle of the kitchen floor. It was the trout fly, made from the kingfisher's crown feather. Mrs. Stark was one step ahead of them. Her foot nearly crushed Meadowsweet as she stooped and picked it up. She held it to the light a moment and snorted with disgust. Then, as Franny and Meadowsweet watched helplessly, she turned, lifted the stove lid again, and tossed it into the flames. Franny thought she saw a tiny puff of blue smoke just before the stove lid clanged down again.

It was deep in the night before Meadowsweet stopped weeping and fell asleep curled up between Diddle and Franny's shoulder.

Chapter Fifteen ⌒

MRS. STARK WAS NASTIER THAN EVER. HER LIPS TWISTED IF Ida mentioned Henry, and the tasks she made her do were even harsher, if possible. Never before had there been such a pressing need to swill out back closets, take up and beat carpets, rub silver, or wash and iron drapes.

One night at dinner, as Mrs. Stark was bringing in the roast, Grandmother said, "Judith, surely there was no need to change all the linens in the spare rooms when we haven't had guests. I think you are asking a bit much of Ida."

Mrs. Stark replied, "Idleness is the root of all evil, Mrs. Morrow. It'll do the girl no harm. Better work than something else . . . And another thing." She looked darkly in Franny's direction. "Ida is a bad influence on the child. She and Henry have been letting her ride the horse *astride*, and we both know that is entirely improper for a young lady. . . ."

Grandmother arched her brows. "Do we, Mrs. Stark? I have always held that it is foolishness to require women to ride sidesaddle. We have legs and we have muscles. I took a very bad fall as a young woman and never rode again. I'm sure it could have been avoided if I'd been allowed to ride as God meant us to. I'm tired of your indecent insinuations, and I beg you to recall that there is a young person present. You are to ease up on Ida. I hope I won't have to warn you again."

Franny looked gratefully at Grandmother. Maybe she wasn't eccentric at all. Maybe she was just sensible. If only she would see Franny, really see her, and talk to her. Grandmother's eyes met hers for a moment. She looked as if she were about to say something, but then her expression clouded and she looked quickly aside.

"Have some meat, Franny?"

Franny sighed and took the platter.

THE NEXT EVENING, SHE NOTICED A BUNCH OF ORANGE flowers in the center of the dining room table when she sat down to dinner. They weren't like any of the usual cut flowers people set on a table. They were beautiful—little speckled, dangling trumpets—but by their thick stalks and broad leaves, they seemed to be some kind of wild weed, not a cultivated plant. What caught Franny's eye were the funny, lumpy little beanlike things that dangled next to some of the blossoms. She couldn't help it, she reached out to touch one. POP! Seeds exploded onto the tablecloth and the pod peeled back in a snakelike curl! Franny drew back as if pricked by a horn-pout's barb. Fascinated, she reached for another, and another. Each behaved in the same astonishing way.

"Magic . . ." she breathed, reaching to touch yet another, not even knowing that she spoke aloud.

"Actually, not," her grandmother said. Franny glanced up to see that Grandmother had been watching her, the tiniest of smiles playing at the corners of her mouth. "It's simply one of nature's extraordinary systems of seed dispersal, though privately I think it's also proof that the creator has a sense of humor. I know of two names for it, jewel weed and touch-me-not. Both are quite apt, I think."

Franny's eyes flashed. "It *is* magic," she said hotly.

Grandmother considered her statement. "Well," she said at length, "you may be right, Franny. There are a lot of words for things we don't understand. Perhaps magic is as good as any."

———•———

THESE DAYS MEADOWSWEET WAS VERY QUIET. FRANNY, Tamarack, and Iris tried to cheer her up, but it was no use. "I was so close to getting that feather," she told them, "so close to flying."

One morning Franny woke to rain thrumming on the roof and a solid gray sky that seemed to have no end of water to pour out of itself. Sea Hag weather, Papa would have said. She and Meadowsweet brought Diddle down to the screened porch and let him play. His tiny claws were amazing. They didn't feel so good on bare skin where he had to dig in to get a grip, but they worked beautifully on stockings and clothing. He could run up and down Franny as if she were a tree. He loved dark places, and would butt his nose under her chin and burrow, tickling horribly, right under her clothes, if she didn't grab him quick enough. Now she let him out of her pocket and he skittered around over the screens and then up onto a beam overhead.

Suddenly there was Meadowsweet down on the ledge, with one of Franny's handkerchiefs stretched across her shoulders, making flapping motions with her arms. Diddle watched her, his head bobbing from side to side, as if he were trying to size up the drop and distance to the ledge.

"Meadowsweet, what are you doing?" cried Franny in alarm. She scrambled up on the table and rescued Diddle before he could launch himself into space.

Meadowsweet plopped down on the ledge. "I was teaching him to fly, Franny. He doesn't have a mama to teach him, so someone's got to," she said crossly.

"Meadowsweet, he's too *liddle*," said Franny, cuddling him under her chin protectively. In answer, Diddle suddenly squirmed free, scooted to the top of Franny's head, and leapt off, flattening himself like a leaf, to sail halfway across the porch before he landed on the floor. His tail twitched, and then he whisked back up the screen and onto the beam again.

Apparently he *was* big enough to fly. Meadowsweet scrambled around wildly, egging him on and squealing with delight. Kingfisher's feather or no, she just couldn't stay sad forever.

After a while, Diddle got hungry and came to his box for some nuts and seeds, but when Franny offered him a dropper full of milk, he pushed it away. When he had eaten, he scuttled into Franny's pocket, burrowed around a moment, and fell asleep.

Franny took a book and curled up on the bearskin rug, but by eleven o'clock, she was tired of reading. Then Franny remembered that she'd never finished exploring the attic after the day she found the kingfisher. Even though the feather had been found, who knew what other treasures might be hidden up there? She slipped the still snoozing squirrel out of her pocket and placed him in his hat nest in his box. Meadowsweet had also fallen asleep, curled up in the bear's fur. Franny carefully tucked her into the hat with Diddle so she would be safe.

Quietly she went upstairs and opened the door to the attic stairs. She wasn't really trying to sneak, but then, she didn't really want to make a lot of noise either. At the top of the stairs she paused and felt in the air for the long string that hung down from the light. She knew it was there, but in the murky gloom, it took a long time of feeling blindly around to find it. Then, at last, her fingers found the metal washer that someone had tied to the end of the string, and she pulled it.

The lighted attic seemed a little more friendly. She stepped over to the shelves full of flat wooden boxes she hadn't examined yet. They had little hooked latches on their sides. She slid one out. It had a glass cover. She saw that inside it, in neat rows, was a collection of beetles, each with a pin stuck carefully through its middle, and a little paper label. Some were very tiny. Others were big and black and pinchy looking. Two of them were a gorgeous, iridescent green, as if they had been painted with enamel.

Franny slid the box back and pulled out another. It was full of tiny butterflies. They were mostly reddish colored. Some of them had completely transparent wings outlined in black. Franny wondered how anyone could have had the patience to identify and arrange them all. The third box took her breath away. It was full of huge butterflies, like nothing she had ever seen before. Several of them were deep purple if she looked at them one way, and glittering blue if she tilted her head. One had scalloped wings with tails and was speckled with velvet black spots over shiny lime green and orange. When she looked closely she saw shimmery golds, reds, and blues too, as if tiny rainbows were somehow hidden on the surface of the wings.

After a long delicious look, she slid that box back into place and pulled out another. In three rows, pins stuck neatly through their bodies, were great brown moths, their wings painted with crescents of rust and edges of pale gold. Some of them had beautiful, fernlike antennae. She pulled out the next box. There was a noise in her ears as if many wings were rushing away in darkness. She began to breathe in ragged gasps. The box contained four large pale green moths with papery wings tapering into long tails, and feathery antennae. The wings were adorned with black and gold eyes. *Tamarack and Iris*, a voice in her heart screamed. But the labels read simply, luna moth: male . . . female . . . spring form . . . summer form . . . They looked faded and very dead.

Franny closed her eyes, as if one of the pins they were impaled on had been driven deep into her own middle. It was all dissolving before her eyes, a whole civilization of magic and wonder, everything she was holding on to, everything she and Papa loved. None of it was real. None of it was magic. There had been no garden fairy. It had been a moth. Tamarack and Iris too. They were all just big green moths.

Franny clenched and unclenched her hands. The kingfisher's gift was just a story. Ida and her little people and her ancient magic were all foolishness. Papa had lied. There were no such things as fairies, and Papa, Papa . . . She closed her eyes against the blackness knifing through her heart.

She found herself flying down the stairs. She threw open the front door, and dashed across the driveway and into the rhododendron thicket. The rain on the big shiny leaves soaked her dress, but she didn't notice. Furiously she kicked and tore at Lakeholm. She was sobbing uncontrollably now. She clawed at the floor of the banquet hall and threw fistfuls of mud and carefully gathered flat stones into the pool. When that destruction was finished, she ran around the side of the house and into the garden. She attacked the tree house castle the same way.

"I hate you! I hate you!" she raged at it, as if it were something alive. Her shoes slipped against the wet bark of the tree. Her dress ripped on a broken branch. She looked at the rope ladder of matchsticks and an idea formed, but the castle, with its little thatched roofs and balconies, was wet with rain.

When everything lay broken in the mud at the base of the tree, she leaned against its living trunk for a moment and felt a flicker of relief in her heart that she hadn't burnt her tree.

Like one in a dream, Franny walked coldly to her room and took out a sheet of writing paper. In harsh black lines she wrote, *You lied to me, Papa, all your fairy people are just lies, and you are dead and never coming back, and I hate you. . . .* But no sooner had she written those words than she tore up the sheet and broke her pencil between her two clenched fists.

Then the blackness came again. There was one more thing to destroy, one more castle built out of all the dead magic. Why should Ida believe in little people and fairy folk who weren't real? She would tell Ida.

Where was she? The kitchen was empty. Then Franny saw that the door to the cellar was open, and she remembered that it was laundry day. She stumbled down the cellar steps, the words wanting to spill out before she even got there. *It's all a lie. It wasn't a fairy. It was just a moth, just a horrible old green moth—*

But she stopped short, mouth open, at the bottom of the

stairs. Ida was hunched, sobbing, over the washtubs, a sheet halfway through the wringer and her hands red and wet from the hot water. Franny stood stock-still. Ida looked at her hopelessly, not even noticing Franny's tangled, wet hair, soaked and torn dress, the mud, the tears, nor that one knee was bleeding. The fury inside Franny drained away suddenly like an ebbing sea. She forgot everything she had been about to say.

"Ida, why are you crying?" she asked.

Ida slumped onto a bench and put her hands up to her face.

"Henry's asked me to marry him."

Franny's numb brain couldn't seem to get around the idea. "But Ida, I thought you loved him," she heard herself say at last. "You seem so happy all the time now with him."

"Oh, Franny, ye don't understand. I do love him, but now that it's come to this I see I am a lying, deceiving person. I canna marry him, and yes, I love him so. Oh, Franny, I shouldna tell you this. It's me babe, me little, little babe . . ." she gasped. "They took him from me. Oh, God, please . . . Franny, you're so young. I'm sorry, I just canna keep it inside." She touched her breast in a hopeless gesture. "Me heart was broken. I couldna bear it."

Then Ida told Franny about handsome Sean O'Connor and his flashing smile, who came nights when she was working at the inn back in Ireland, and who did "whist" her away. How she'd caught her breath just to look at the handsomeness of him: square shoulders, slim, with hair like burnished copper, and eyes like the summer sky, and oh, how he could dance—with that smile flashing like sunlight on the bay. And when she knew it was for her . . . Even his hands touching the linen of her apron were beautiful. He'd said, he'd said, that they would marry . . . that she was lovely like a rose, sure, and he would marry her when the roses bloomed. . . .

"But he didn't, Franny. The time came and went again. At Caitlin Flannery's wedding, he danced with Caitlin's little sister. Danced and danced, with eyes going blank if they roved past me, with the white rose pinned hopefully at me throat. Later I ripped that rose apart and left it torn on the road home for hooves and boots and rain to trample into the mud.

"When I knew I was with child, I went once to the farm meaning to tell him, but he was there, lounging at the well, chewing a straw while he watched the dairymaid draw her buckets. I knew then that I didna want him. But what was I to do? So I sent off a letter to me uncle in Boston, full of lies about how I was taken with America, and couldn't he find a position for me with a good family. I was a hard worker, let him write Mrs. Black at the inn.

"One day the return letter came. Mother was home then and stronger. I left me family and me home with that secret inside me. And oh, Franny, the sick, weary, gray days crossing the Atlantic. It was a wonder I didna lose the child then. But later in me uncle's house, when he knew—the anger—and Aunt Margaret said, 'They'll take it at the foundling home, and the world will be none the wiser'—as if he were a stolen sack of potatoes, Franny, and not part of me own flesh and soul.

"I was frightened and alone. When the baby came, I touched him in wonder, he was so lovely. But everything was decided. Next morning when I awoke, he was gone. They took care of that for me. Not even a good-bye, not a snippet of hair or the blanket from him. And now I must tell Henry the truth about meself and he'll not want me. Ah, Franny, he'll not want me."

Franny put a tentative hand on Ida's arm. She wasn't sure if she understood everything Ida had told her, but somehow, she knew there was nothing for her to say. It was Ida's belief in the fairy that had opened her eyes to Henry. She couldn't be the one to tell her it wasn't real. Not now. Not when Ida needed magic so much. Ida flinched at the touch of Franny's hand, then buried her head on Franny's shoulder. In the musty shadows of the cellar they sat while the grief flowed. Franny wished Papa were there. He would have known what to do.

Suddenly there were sounds above them on the landing outside the kitchen door. Someone had been listening and didn't much care if they knew. There were heavy footsteps, then the door to the kitchen opened and closed with a bang, and they knew that Mrs. Stark had heard every word that had been said. Ida and Franny stared at each other in horror.

Chapter Sixteen ⌒

FRANNY POUNDED UP THE STAIRS AND FOUND MRS. STARK confronting Grandmother in the hallway. It was as if the housekeeper had turned into some sort of demon with all her poison and meanness boiling out. Her face was twisted into something halfway between a snarl and a thin sneer of triumph. A vein bulged across her forehead, her nostrils curled, yet her lips were drawn back over her teeth in a freezing sort of grin. Her voice rasped and broke more than ever as she stood, hands on hips, telling the whole thing to Grandmother, just as she had overheard Ida telling Franny in the cellar.

"She's no better than a harlot, Mrs. Morrow, a common . . ."

"Mrs. Stark, please." Grandmother raised her eyebrows and looked meaningfully in Franny's direction.

"That's all right. The child knows every sordid detail. That girl saw fit to tell her. I was minding my work, sorting fruit jars, and I heard it all."

Franny felt herself slowly going on fire in every nerve.

Grandmother stood straight as a little tree. She seemed to be looking intently at one of her birds, a magnificently colored yellow-shafted flicker, which guarded a nest cavity in a section of oak standing in the alcove by the front door. Franny's brain felt frozen. She couldn't think what to do.

Grandmother would send Ida away. Henry would go back to lonesome evenings reading automobile journals by his window, and Ida would scrub pots in someone else's kitchen, soundlessly, forever. Franny would never again hear that sweet breathy singing in Grandmother's hallway or the tapping of Ida's feet as she danced to the swirl of Henry's pennywhistle.

"Grandmother, please . . ." Franny started to say, but Grandmother turned away from her without speaking and walked out to her garden.

Franny went to Ida's room. She knocked softly on the door and Ida let her come in. She was putting her few things into a small cracked leather valise. Franny saw that she had already emptied the jar on her dresser of its bunch of wildflowers and thrown them into the wastebasket.

"I have to go, Franny. Your grandmother can't keep the likes of me, not now, knowin' me past."

Franny didn't know what to say. She watched as Ida took her little picture of Saint Patrick from the wall and her Bible from the dresser, wrapped them carefully in paper, and packed them. It didn't take long. Ida placed the valise by the door. It looked lonely and a long way from Ireland or anyplace that she could call home.

Then Ida took her black coat from its hanger in the closet and laid it over the valise. She picked up a little white box from the nightstand and held it in her hands. Franny knew it held the ring that Henry had given her. She sat down stiffly and looked with dry eyes at Franny. Franny fell into her arms, choking out, "Where will you go? What will happen to you?"

Ida held Franny close a moment, stroking her hair, murmuring, "You were just like me little sister Eileen."

"But what about Henry, Ida? He loves you. He wants to marry you—he bought you a ring."

Ida's mouth quivered and the rigidity went out of her body suddenly. She looked limp and scared. "I deceived him, Franny. I didna tell him of no Sean O'Connor, or babe. . . . And now I've lost him—a man far better. I've nothing now. . . ." Her voice trailed off into a whisper, and she began to rock herself. Franny thought of the crazy woman she once saw on a bench in the park in Boston on a cold winter day. She had sat rocking herself and staring, as Ida did now. Franny felt a sickness in the pit of her stomach. Not Ida. Not her Ida, who could be so full of music and life.

Suddenly Franny was angry again. She backed away from Ida and took off running to find Grandmother. She found her standing in the front hall, talking again to Mrs. Stark. "Could you please tell Henry to come here?" Grandmother said in a tight voice. Mrs. Stark went.

Grandmother turned and was hit by a ferocious Franny,

tears streaming, face white under her freckles. "You can't send Ida away! It isn't fair, Grandmother. She has nowhere to go. I won't let you!"

The old woman took Franny by the wrists with surprising strength, but still Franny was nearly too much for her. It was only by the command of her voice that she got her under control.

"Hush, Franny. What's happened to you? Who said anything about sending Ida away?"

Franny stood trembling, her ribs heaving. "But why do you want Henry? You'll tell him about Ida and make her go away!"

Grandmother stared beyond Franny a moment, seeming to gather herself together. Then she looked at Franny very hard. "Henry and his wife, Sarah, were childless nearly ten years before she died," she said in a low voice. "Ida might never have another baby. You understand that, don't you, Franny? I've known Henry a long time and I know how good-hearted he is. If he's willing, I'm going to the orphanage to fetch back Ida's baby—that is, if he's not been adopted yet."

Franny struggled to grasp what Grandmother was saying. Mama, and Nana DiCrista, or any other grown-up Franny knew, would never think of such a thing. An unmarried woman's child was not even to be spoken of, except in shocked whispers. Such a woman was called wicked and sinful, and there was a horrible name for the child. But Ida wasn't wicked, and how could a baby be anything but good? It was lying Sean O'Connor who was wicked.

She didn't know if she understood about Henry and his first wife or not. Mama never discussed such things as babies. But Franny remembered Mr. B scolding the old tatter-eared tomcat for "makin' too many leetle tommycats." She knew that some women could not bear children, and she knew somehow that you needed a father to get babies. What if some men couldn't make babies? What if Henry . . . Franny returned her grandmother's look with one equally determined.

"I'm coming with you," she said.

Grandmother drew in her breath. "All right," she said at last, "but first I must talk to Henry. In the meantime, don't say anything about this to Ida. We may not find the child still there. And Franny," she added, "you look as if you'd been through a cyclone. I think you'd best change into clean, dry clothes and brush your hair."

Chapter Seventeen ∼

It seemed a long drive to the orphanage in Boston. Franny wondered at herself. An hour ago, everything had been so black. Now it was all different. So much was shattered, but somehow there was a big, shimmering bubble of hope inside her. Something very real and wonderful might happen. She and Grandmother were going to try to make it happen. Once Franny looked at Grandmother and started to ask, "Why did you . . . ?"

But Grandmother silenced her with a look and a shake of her head. "Some things are best not spoken of," she said. The old woman gazed out the window of the car, and once again Franny imagined that Grandmother had somehow shut herself behind glass. *Something in life must have hurt her once. . . .*

In the driver's seat, Henry attended perfectly to his business, but there was something different about the way he gripped the wheel and stared at the road. They entered a part of Boston that Franny had never seen before. The rain had stopped, but the sky was a sullen gray. The city steamed wetly, and the heavy air was so full of a mixture of smells—horses, cars, refuse, smoke—that Franny could almost taste it. The buildings here sagged slightly and looked blackened. Some brownish-looking laundry hung limply on lines across the alleyways.

Then they turned in at a gate and pulled up in front of a brick building that somehow looked chilly even in the August heat. It had few windows and the ones it had looked hazy and blind, like Lady's eyes. The orphanage crouched between the buildings on each side of it, almost as if it were shivering.

Henry parked and walked around to Grandmother's door and opened it for her very formally, offering her his arm. Grandmother accepted his help and stepped out.

"I don't know how long we'll be, Henry."

Franny scrambled out behind her. Just as formally, Henry offered Franny his arm, and as he did so, his eyes met hers. There was a funny look in them, almost as if he were asking for something. Franny tried to smile back at him.

A flock of children were playing in a bare dirt yard at a swing set and seesaws. They fell silent and stared at the car and at Franny and Grandmother walking past them to the front door. Franny's cheeks burned. The children were not dressed in rags, and they were fairly clean, but their clothing had the same brownish, worn look of the lines of laundry and build-ings around them. She realized how fine her neatly starched and ironed dress, polished shoes, and clean stockings must look to these children. They were orphans. They had no papa or mama, not even a grandmother to take them in. For just a moment, Franny thought about her mother in Europe, and her heart thudded in her chest. Did she miss Franny, or was she having gowns fitted, dancing, and finding a new husband to take Papa's place? Stubbornly, Franny shut out the thought of Mama.

In a corner of the yard, a skinny black girl was on her knees pulling weeds from a little patch of garden. She was minding a red-haired baby, who sat on the ground beside a big wooden barrel. He was playing in the mud with a short stick, and though he was not old enough to walk, he seemed very intent on what he was doing.

Could he possibly be Ida's baby? Franny wondered what the barrel was for. Was it used to collect rainwater? She stared at the garden. She could see that Grandmother was staring at it too. It was so alive! Franny recognized bluish cabbage leaves, bright green lettuce, and trailing squash vines. It was so unexpected in this barren place.

As they watched, Franny heard the cry of a ragman, the creak of his wagon, and the hollow clop of his horse's hooves coming up the street. The skinny girl stared at it so hard that Franny looked too. Just before turning into the next street, the horse lifted its tail and manured with a splat onto the wet cobbles. The girl's face broke into a grin. She scooped up the baby and plunked him safely in the barrel—that's what it was for! Then she snatched a battered pail and shovel, picked up her skirts, and ran to collect the manure.

Grandmother smiled as the girl dumped her pail onto what looked like a heap of dirt and garbage next to her garden. "That's a compost pile," she explained to Franny. "She knows better than to put fresh manure on the plants. But would you believe such resourcefulness?"

Once inside the orphanage, Grandmother drew herself up so straight that the feathers in her hat quivered, and spoke to the woman at the receiving desk. "We are looking for a certain child that was left here last November. . . ."

The woman blinked watery eyes and nodded as Grandmother gave her the information. Her nose and hands were so red they looked sore. She sniffed and began slowly to search through a large file drawer. She wiped her nose with the hem of her apron. Franny began to feel impatient. She could hear the sound of a baby crying from somewhere upstairs. Maybe that was Ida's baby!

She looked back to where the watery-eyed woman was still searching her files. She wished she would hurry up. Finally the woman sniffed once again and shook her head.

"There's no file showing we still have this child, and no record of adoption. Excuse me a minute." She vanished into another room. Grandmother sat down in a chair. Franny shuffled her feet impatiently.

Finally she heard the door open behind her.

"I'm sorry, Mrs. Morrow. The child in question died of diphtheria at two months of age. We lost quite a few of the poor little dears, though who's to say they're not better off with their maker." The words fell like bars of iron and seemed to echo in the room.

Franny felt blackness seeping into her brain like ink on a blotter. She saw Grandmother's shoulders droop. There was a long time when no one said anything. Then Grandmother finally said, in a strangled voice, "Well, I guess that's that. Come along, Franny, we'd best go."

Franny's eyes blurred. It was all swimming in front of her, all confusion, something wonderful draining away, slipping, going . . . Grandmother turned and walked outside. Franny followed, trying not to stumble. She could see that Grandmother's shoulders were straight again, but looking at her from the back, Franny saw something defeated about her that made her think of General Lee and Traveller. Grandmother started slowly, and, Franny thought, a little unsteadily back toward Henry waiting in the car. As they passed a bench, she suddenly put out a hand, caught herself, and sat down. Franny saw that she was weeping.

It seemed unbearable that Grandmother should do that. Uncertainly Franny took Grandmother's hand. "Don't cry," she said, but she wanted to cry herself. Suddenly Grandmother took Franny in her arms, and Franny, who had never hugged her grandmother before, clung to her the way she used to cling to Papa when the sky was too full of thunder and lightning.

"Oh, Franny, I've been so wrong to you, so foolish. Sometimes I wanted to reach out to you, sometimes I tried, but then I would remember my own little girl, and the pain was too much. I was trying to protect myself. Then, when this happened with Ida, I thought I could fix things, but it was my own long ago past I was trying to fix. How could I possibly think I could repair the lives of two other people?" She took a delicately embroidered handkerchief from her purse and laughed a small, hollow laugh. Then more tears rolled down the fine lines of her cheeks. She looked at Franny hopelessly.

"Franny, when I was young, I fell in love with a naturalist. My parents would not allow us to marry, as he had no financial prospects. Who knows, perhaps they were right. It might have been a hard life for me. But the problem was, I was pregnant. I was sent to cousins in Europe, where I had my baby at a Swiss hospital. She was given away. . . ." Here Grandmother's voice broke. Franny felt some of the swirling in her head begin to stop. She knew she should be shocked at Grandmother, but she wasn't.

Grandmother continued. "A year later I was married to your grandfather. He was a successful lumberman and a good husband and father. In time, I came to love him very much. But the part of me that collects things, and walks, and observes nature, never stopped loving Martin and our little lost girl. I was glad that James and I had sons. I always shied away from little girls. . . .

"Franny, sometimes a woman chooses to give her child away. That is a very strong kind of love, because sometimes it is for the best. If loving parents are found for the child, that is a kind of magic. But if a woman is able to care for her child and loves him, no one should take him away from her."

With stiff-fingered difficulty, Grandmother took the chain and locket from around her neck and put it into Franny's hand. "Open it, Franny. I can't seem to manage my fingers well enough now to do it myself."

Franny slipped her thumbnail under the catch. The tiny heart opened to reveal a snip of black hair softer to the touch than any paintbrush. Grandmother stroked it with an unsteady fingertip, looked at it a long time, then closed the locket with a sigh and sat with it clasped in her hand. "I wonder what her life is like," she murmured.

Then she straightened and looked at Franny intently. "Now, Franny, do you see why I could not bear to see Ida's child taken from her when it was not necessary? Perhaps it makes me an outlaw in our world, but I've had many years to think over what happened to me. It was not necessary or right. Children are given to us for love and joy only." Here she touched Franny's cheek softly.

Franny looked at Grandmother, and the old woman's eyes seemed to have lost their uncertain color. They were clear green, fairy green. There was no glass barrier, no formal stiffness in the look. Franny knew suddenly that the barrier between them was gone forever. She felt some of the blackness fading away.

Grandmother held Franny closely. "I've been living in a shell. When your mother kept you away from me, I didn't

160

argue with her. I thought I could never love another little girl—until now. I see how foolish I have been. And you are very like your father. There is indeed some great mystery in life."

"But no magic, no fairies," said Franny bitterly. Then she told Grandmother about Papa's stories, the Tamarack family, Ida's little folk, and the real fairy that was nothing but a moth.

Grandmother leaned back and smiled faintly. "And the world is a hard and cold place, you hate moths, you feel like a fool, and you want to tell Ida, don't you?"

Franny nodded fiercely. "And Ida's baby is dead, and my papa is dead and my mother doesn't like stories and loves dresses more than me, and I should go and live in the orphanage and die of diphtheria. . . .

"But I couldn't tell Ida about the moth, Grandmother, not ever. It was because she believed America had little people, like Ireland does, that she came to life again and saw that Henry loves her."

Grandmother handed Franny her handkerchief and Franny blew her nose wetly. Then in a voice that had all the warmth and softness of Bobby Burns and the bearskin rug, Grandmother said, "Listen to me, Franny, you did the right thing. But what of Tamarack and Iris and Meadowsweet? How do you know that they are not real, just because a moth is not a fairy? They have stayed with you, as I understand fairies do when they are needed. I don't think that you must part with them now—or ever. People are entirely too narrow-minded about what is real and what isn't. There are spirits around us in the flowers, the trees, even in the rocks, and especially in animals and people. I can't say that there are not such things as fairies and magic, but I do know that sometimes we have to make our own magic.

"Ida comes from a land and a tradition of old magic. Even if you were to tell her about the moth, she might not believe you, and what good would it accomplish? The moths in the box are dead. They were collected for study. But no dead thing can even faintly resemble the charged beauty of one of God's living creations. Franny, sometime you must look again, with open eyes, at your living moth."

Grandmother's voice was tired now. "There is joy in life, and a great deal of pain. We must go home now and try to look toward the joy and beauty in life. We must do our best to accept what we cannot change."

Franny stared at the bare ground in front of her for a long time, thinking. Then, over by the little square of garden, the baby began to wail just the way Meadowsweet did when she was caught in the spider's web. The girl picked him up, put him on one skinny hip, and began to dance, singing a rhythmic little song. Franny couldn't hear what she was singing, but the last word that Grandmother had said, *change*, seemed to repeat itself inside her head, in time with the rhythm of the song: *change, change* . . . and suddenly Franny knew what to do. Maybe some things could never be changed, but hadn't

Grandmother also said that sometimes you could make your own magic?

"A changeling, Grandmother," she said.

Grandmother looked at her blankly.

"Ida's baby can be a changeling. Tamarack and Iris love Meadowsweet just as much, and she isn't really their own baby."

"What do you mean, child? Ida's baby is dead."

"No," said Franny more firmly. "He's not, I mean, he doesn't need to be. Ida had him for only a few hours. She hardly saw him. Would she know what he looks like? There are babies here who need mothers and fathers. Then Henry could have a son. We could make magic, Grandmother."

Franny's grandmother sat motionless, staring at Franny. Suddenly life seemed to flow back into her. A light flickered in her green eyes and she laughed a wonderful, tiny laugh that seemed to float in the air. Together they looked over to the garden at the baby in the girl's arms. Grandmother rose and Franny followed.

———•———

THE GIRL GLANCED AT THEM WARILY AS THEY APPROACHED. "He's a lovely little boy," Grandmother said kindly. "Suppose someone were to adopt him?"

A look of fear flashed for an instant across the girl's face, and her dark hand tightened on the baby's thigh, but just as quickly, she took a breath and straightened her shoulders. "It's what I hope and pray for every day, ma'am," she answered, looking squarely at Grandmother. "He's such a good boy, an' real smart. I draws things in the dirt for him an' he tries to copy them already. But them ladies don't have time to play wit him so I keep him wit me much as I kin."

The baby looked at Grandmother with solemn eyes and suddenly reached for the feather in her hat. Grandmother smiled. She took off the hat, removed the white plume, and gave it to him. "It's a snowy egret's feather," she told him as if he could understand. "I wear it only because it was a gift from my mother. Too many have been taken and Florida must not be without egrets, but isn't it lovely?"

Franny thought he agreed about the feather, because he began to chew the airy down. The girl distracted him by pulling a string of buttons from her pocket. He accepted the change without much fuss, fingering one of the large buttons while she returned the feather to Grandmother.

Then Grandmother asked, "How old is this little boy?"

"He be 'most nine months."

Grandmother looked quickly at Franny, then back to the girl. "What if I told you his mother was forced to leave him here, but now that she has secure employment she is able to take him back?"

"I be surprised because I was told his mother die when he born."

"In a way she did," said Grandmother quietly. "Now what

if I told you that having this baby would bring back life and happiness to her and he would be loved and well cared for?"

"Then I don' ask no questions, or say nothin', I just be happy my prayers is answered. It be all right for me. I had my ma and pa 'most until I could take care of myself. But a baby need a ma and pa, or at least one or th' other." She looked down and bit her lip. "But I be sad to say good-bye to Billy. . . ."

Grandmother looked thoughtfully at the garden. "You do well to grow such plants in this bare ground," she said.

The girl smiled a little. "I was raised on a farm until I lost my folks. My ma showed me. It was a lotta work choppin' the ground at first. Once I got it worked up, it wasn't so bad. They let me take sprouted potatoes from the cellar to plant in the spring, and when I get a little money I buy seeds. They's real glad fer what I kin grow. I make some of the other big kids help me. They all need the greens an' stuff." There was a note of pride in her voice.

Grandmother's next question astonished Franny. "Young woman, can you cook?" she asked.

The girl didn't blink. "I never cooked much, but I learn faster than a skinned cat. I kin do whatever I have to if it means living."

"Maybe you don't need to say good-bye to Billy. If you are old enough to go out and work, I have a place for you." Grandmother turned to Franny. "I think I have killed two birds with one stone, though of course we both know I don't kill birds anymore!" she said with a laugh.

Chapter Eighteen ◡

It was hard to leave the baby behind, but inquiries must be made, papers signed, regulations followed. There was nothing for it but that they must wait two weeks for the adoption to be approved. Meanwhile nothing must be said to Ida, except that she must not go away.

"But someone else must leave at once," added Grandmother grimly in the car on the way home. "I had not realized what a black cloud on our lives Mrs. Stark has become. And Henry, perhaps it would be best for now not to let on to Ida that you know anything about her child."

———•———

Franny couldn't help it. She listened shamelessly at the study door when Grandmother dismissed Mrs. Stark.

"You have always been such a good manager, I couldn't rationalize letting you go before, but you have finally shown your true colors," Grandmother said in a tight, controlled tone. "You are a cruel and spiteful woman. I wonder what can have made you that way."

"I've done no more than the duty of any God-fearing woman," retorted Mrs. Stark, her voice rasping like fingernails on slate. "I'm well rid of this house with its filthy animals, your Irish shanty girl of a maid, and your sneaking, deluded grandchild."

Franny heard Grandmother's chair scrape back suddenly. Her words seemed to vibrate with fury. "I will not dignify that speech with a response. You will leave this house first thing in the morning." Franny danced upstairs before she could be caught.

———•———

WHEN SHE WENT TO CHECK ON DIDDLE BEFORE BED, HE was out of his box. There was a small hole in the corner of one of the screens on the porch. Maybe he and Meadowsweet were out in the garden playing. Franny didn't worry too much. She knew he would come back to eat. After all, flying squirrels usually slept all day and stayed awake at night, and he was almost grown up. She noticed that Stripesy, who often slept in Diddle's box, was gone too. She looked under the woolen hat. Then she saw a neat brown cocoon, like a tiny furry egg, in the corner of the box. "Oh, Stripesy . . ." she murmured.

———•———

The next morning Mrs. Stark's fat black suitcase appeared on the steps by the kitchen door. It was taken away by Henry, driving the Cadillac, with a granite-faced Sea Hag sitting in the back. She left without a word for those who saw her off.

Ida had been persuaded to stay. "The only thing I need to know about you is that you are a hard worker and an honest person," Grandmother had said firmly to her. "Besides, if anyone expects me to learn to cook or do ironing at sixty-seven years of age, they had best be ready to watch the house burn down! I'll be needing you, young lady."

As soon as Mrs. Stark was gone, Franny went out to the garden and timidly pulled back the branches of the mulberry tree. Her heart ached, seeing what she had done. There was no sign of Tamarack, Iris, or Meadowsweet. Wearily she dragged herself up into the arms of the tree and laid her cheek on the rough bark. A tear slid out from under an eyelid. How could she ever have done such a thing to her friends? They would never come back.

But then she felt a familiar tugging on her earlobe. "Wake up, stupid, so I can kick you!" said Meadowsweet. Franny opened her eyes.

"Meadowsweet!" Then she saw Tamarack and Iris sitting calmly on a bit of remaining floorboard. "Oh, how can you ever forgive me?" she whispered. "I smashed your beautiful houses, both of them. I'm so sorry."

"Well, we're pretty sorry too," began Meadowsweet indignantly, but her mother stopped her.

"Meadowsweet, she feels bad enough, you don't need to rub it in," said Iris. She started down the twisted remains of a ladder toward Franny. Her skirt became momentarily tangled and after she tugged the hollyhock ruffle free, she said, "Oh, bother!" and fluttered the rest of the way over to Franny's lap. "Franny," she said, patting her hand reassuringly with little pats that felt like dry raindrops, "I don't believe it was you at all doing what you did. I believe it was something big and dark in your life, something that we all fight with at some point, that did it. Anyway, a house is easy to repair compared with a little girl's heart. We're glad that your heart is better."

Tamarack was beside Iris now, with his arm around Meadowsweet, who seemed to be almost over her crossness. "Anyway, Franny, you'll be going back to Cambridge soon, and I'm not sure you'll still be needing us." He looked at Franny closely, as if trying to see how she would take it. Somehow Franny wasn't surprised. Somehow she knew. Tamarack seemed satisfied with what he saw in Franny's face. "We've been thinking of relocating to the old Larch Tree Mansion," he said. He glanced at Iris, who nodded calmly. "We'd like to stay in the neighborhood because you'll be coming back here often now, I think—and besides, there will be somebody small here soon who may need us sometime." Franny knew he was talking about Ida's baby.

"I've come to realize that Meadowsweet is growing up," explained Iris, smiling at her daughter. "I've just got to trust that a water sprite knows how to navigate the dangers of the water realm. It's a lovely place, and she'll be happier living near a real body of water."

"And Franny, I never told anyone, but I saw my changeling sister," said Meadowsweet, her eyes sparkling. "She helped me find Diddle under the water. We can fly underwater together!"

"But you'll never fly in the air," said Franny sadly. Meadowsweet tried to look properly sorry for herself, but she couldn't quite do it. The corners of her mouth started twitching and a little gleam came into her eyes.

"What is it, Meadowsweet?" asked Iris suspiciously.

Meadowsweet stood up, pursed her lips, and gave a tiny, piercing whistle. There was a scuffling from the cigar box in the branches overhead (it had survived Franny's storm), and a little whiskered face blinked sleepily down at them.

"Diddle!" exclaimed Franny. "So that's where you've been!"

"Watch this," said Meadowsweet. She whistled more commandingly, and Diddle scuttled down through the branches to her. Meadowsweet gave him a kiss on the nose, then wrapped her arms around his neck and whispered, "Go!" The little squirrel instantly raced to the top of the tree, with Meadowsweet clinging to his back.

"Oh!" gasped Iris, clutching Tamarack's arm. Then she clapped her hands over her mouth.

"I think she knows what she's doing," Tamarack reassured her.

When Diddle reached the very topmost branch, Meadowsweet whispered, "Go!" again to him. He nodded his head from side to side a moment, planning his glide, then suddenly spread his cape of loose skin and flew, between the branches, in a long smooth arc to the ground. Meadowsweet clung to his back like he was some sort of living, water sprite–size bearskin rug. When they landed, she hugged him, laughing, and cried, "See! I *can* fly!"

Diddle scampered to the top of the tree again, and the next time, Iris and Tamarack flew alongside Meadowsweet and Diddle. Three more times they flew for Franny, until they were all breathless and laughing with the excitement of it. Then suddenly, Diddle yawned and skittered up into Franny's lap, looking for her pocket. She stroked his soft fur as he curled up to go to sleep again.

"I guess you'd rather stay here with Meadowsweet than live in Cambridge," she said softly to him. She swallowed and her voice broke a little. "And Meadowsweet's going to miss Stripesy so much as it is. You can always count on Grandmother for food. She doesn't care whether she feeds birds or squirrels. And I will come visit all of you—a lot."

Chapter Nineteen ≥

ONE MORNING, AS FRANNY AND GRANDMOTHER WERE
returning from a walk to the orchard to check on the bluebird
fledglings, the telephone rang. Grandmother stepped over to
it and lifted the receiver on its cord. "Could you say that
again?" she said into the mouthpiece. "Well, that's splendid.
They'll be so pleased. Yes, we'll come directly."

When Grandmother hung up the receiver again and turned
to Franny, her eyes were like misty stars and her cheeks were
as pink as her roses. "Well, child, we've done it. Ida and Henry
shall have their child! And I'm to have a new cook, though I
daresay we may have to settle for a scorched roast or two while
she's learning her art."

So it was that Henry, Grandmother, and Franny made a
second trip to the orphanage. When they returned, they found
Ida in the kitchen taking a loaf of soda bread out of the oven.
She had hardly spoken to Henry during the past two weeks,
but he had borne it patiently. "I hope it was a successful shop-

ping trip you and Franny had, ma'am," she said, returning her pot holders to their hook.

"Ida, we must talk," said Grandmother, taking off her gloves in a businesslike way.

Ida looked questioningly at Grandmother. Franny heard the door open quietly behind them as Henry stepped inside. In his arms he carried the child, who sniffed and hiccuped. There had been some crying in the car. The girl, Sylva, followed, carrying her things in a flour sack and looking curiously around. Franny thought that for a man who had never had a baby of his own, Henry seemed to know how to hold this one pretty well. He looked shy and sure, both at the same time, and she thought she would always remember the sight of him standing in the kitchen doorway bringing Ida her baby. She heard Ida's quick intake of breath.

Grandmother said quite coolly, "We shall say that you were widowed in Ireland. Your child was left in the care of an aunt in Boston. Now that you have established yourself here, you have sent for your child to join you. Happily, you have fallen in love again. I don't believe your marriage will be questioned." There was something about her tone that made Franny feel certain that no one would dare question the marriage of Grandmother Morrow's maid. "No one has the right to tear a child from its mother," Grandmother added, almost to herself.

She left them, a strange light of triumph in her eyes, to

show Sylva where to put her things. Then she went to sit in her rose garden until nearly dusk.

Ida stood frozen, her hands clenched at her sides as if she were using all her strength to keep them there. "I'm so sorry . . ." she began, but Henry stopped her. He said nothing, but put the little boy into her arms and then his own long arms around the two of them. Franny seemed to wake up then, and knew enough to fade quietly out of the room.

That evening, Grandmother smiled warmly at Franny over a supper of cold meat and bread and butter that they had rummaged together out of the icebox. "I won't ask that young woman to start learning to cook tonight," said Grandmother. "She's a bit overwhelmed." It seemed to Franny like the nicest meal she had ever had at Grandmother's house. The house might be full of changes, but her heart felt calm. There was something about the way Grandmother looked at her and seemed not only to see her, but to listen to what she had to say, that made Franny think Grandmother felt peaceful as well.

IDA SAID IT WAS THE LITTLE PEOPLE WHO HAD BROUGHT her such great good fortune. How else could it be explained that her life should suddenly be mended and whole? Mr. B's wife sent over clothes from her grandchildren for both Sylva and the baby. Grandmother produced a knitted white wool blanket that had long ago been Franny's father's.

Henry and Ida were given time off to get to know their child. Sylva was only too glad to share all she knew about him and help Ida when he was fussy. She took to her new kitchen work like a small hurricane. Ida had never had a chance to name her boy. The name he came with from the orphanage, Billy, was quietly changed to George Henry. It didn't take long for him to learn to wrap his arms around Ida's neck and say "Mama."

He was big-eyed and solemn, but not unresponsive. Franny loved to sit with him in Ida's room and show him seashells or roll a ball back and forth with him. One day, as she was cuddling him in her lap, she found herself starting to tell him a story: "Once upon a time there was a fairy prince named Tamarack. He was so small that he could ride on the back of his friend, a slate-blue kingfisher named Skyfeather. . . ."

Henry and Ida were to be married in late September. Franny's mother would be home from Europe by then, and Franny would have started at school again in Cambridge. She hoped that her mother would let her come back for the wedding. Suddenly the thought of leaving Grandmother's house pulled at her heart.

If a child seemed an unusual feature to an engagement, Henry did not seem in the least put off. He came often to sit at the kitchen table, spoon feeding cereal to little "Hank." Ida watched with a never ending light of amazement in her eye. Surely, surely, the pale green fairy had brought magic.

<hr />

IT WAS NEARLY TEN O'CLOCK ONE NIGHT WHEN GRAND-mother tapped on Franny's door. She wore a light blue satin wrapper over her nightdress. Her braids hanging down her shoulders and the warm glow from the candle she carried made her almost young looking. "I thought we might look for the green fairy," she said simply. She held out her shawl and wrapped Franny in it. It was almost the end of the month, and the night was a little cool.

Together they crept past the grandfather clock and the glass-eyed owl, down the stairs past the silent little birds in their jars, through the dining room, and out to the screened porch. They must not wake Ida or the baby. Carefully Grand-mother lighted the oil lamp and they settled into the wicker chairs to wait. The moon had risen full and high, so that the small world of the garden seemed alive in the light of some cool, distant sun.

The air was full of movement and scents that Franny couldn't quite name. A rhythmic hooting floated up from the orchard. "Barred owl," remarked Grandmother. Franny thought of the indigo bunting and yellowthroat warbler Grandmother had shown her on their walk to the orchard. She smiled to herself. There *were* exotic jewel birds in these ordi-nary Massachusetts woods.

The minutes stretched out. No luna moth came. Franny shifted restlessly in her chair.

"Franny," Grandmother whispered, leaning toward her,

"what do you say we get Mr. B to hitch Bobby Burns up to the buggy tomorrow and see if he remembers the old Reservoir Road? Have you ever seen a great blue heron rookery? I've got a notion to do a little jouncing and feel the reins in my hands. Would you like to learn to drive?"

Franny looked at Grandmother, surprise and pleasure on her face. "Yes, please. I mean, yes, I'd love it!"

There was a long silence. Then Grandmother spoke again. "Franny?" Grandmother's voice was hesitant.

"What, Grandmother?"

"Franny, I believe every mother loves her child. I think your mother is just jealous of the wonderful relationship you had with your papa."

Franny began to cry silently. Grandmother continued, "She was foolish. It was unforgivable to burn your papa's stories. She never could understand that I was supportive of his writing." Here Grandmother's eyes met Franny's and there was suddenly a warmth between them such as Franny had not felt with anyone since Papa died. "Franny, you must give your mother another chance. You must forgive her. See how Ida loves her boy? Once you were tiny like Hank, and your mother held you like a little precious doll."

Franny didn't speak for a long time. At last she turned to Grandmother and said, "I remember Papa's stories. Someday I will write them again for him."

Grandmother nodded, tears filling her eyes. "Yes, Franny,

but more important, you must write your own stories. I've no doubt in the world but what your head is filled to the brim with them."

There still was no moth, and Franny dozed. But she woke with a start to Grandmother's hand lightly on her arm, and a fluttering shadow on the screen. Quietly Franny stood up. The great moth lifted off into the shadows of the mulberry tree. Franny looked at Grandmother and the old woman nodded to her. Franny stepped to the door and let herself out onto the damp lawn. Where had it gone? Her eyes searched the blue shadows. It was dancing back to the screen. It wanted the light and moved restlessly, seeking a way to get closer to it. Then it paused, and Franny found herself just inches away. The tissue-thin wings were lighted by the lamplight from one side, and shimmered with reflected sun-moonlight on the other.

Franny felt her head begin to swim. Her eyes were seeing a green so pale, yet alive, it seemed to glow with an inner light. This was so different from the faded dead things in the attic box. How could one ever explain without seeing with one's own eyes? Luna, moth of the moon. The body was soft, womanly, clothed in white velvet as a queen of fairies should be. The antennae were like delicate fronds, seeking, tasting unseen vibrations and scents. The jewel-like eyes on each wing stared eerily. The wings fluttered like skirts of cobweb silk, sulphur colored at their margins, and tapering into trailing tails. What, thought Franny suddenly, in the most wonderful imagining, could be more lovely and mysterious than this creature?

She turned slightly to find her grandmother beside her. Their eyes met—Grandmother's questioning, Franny's radiant.

Chapter Twenty ❧

Dear Papa,

This morning Ida and Henry were married. Henry drove out to Cambridge yesterday specially to bring me. I got to hold Hank during the ceremony and boy, did he squirm. I had my basket all filled with rose petals too. I couldn't hold them both, so I put it on the seat beside me. Tamarack, Iris, and Meadowsweet sat right among the rose petals and watched. But we left Diddle at home, sleeping in his cigar box. He's never awake now in the daytime anyway.

Ida was so beautiful. She wore a linen suit the color of a dove. Grandmother picked her a bouquet of late roses from her garden. Henry looked kind of funny in his suit, as if he couldn't bend or something, but he held Ida's hand like she was a princess.

Halfway through the ceremony, Hank wanted his mama and began to cry. I didn't know what to do.

Sylva was beside me. She's a little less skinny now, and looked pretty in a pink dress that Ida had made for her. She kept stroking the fabric. I don't think she had ever had a dress like that before. Anyway, Sylva fished a biscuit and Hank's string of buttons out of her pocket, but he wouldn't even look at them.

Then Meadowsweet climbed out of the basket and scrambled up on my shoulder. Hank got really quiet and just stared at her. Meadowsweet stood up and danced a little dance for him. Hank put his thumb in his mouth and stared some more. Then she put her hands in front of her eyes, and played peek-a-boo! Hank giggled. She did it again, and he put his hands up to his own eyes and tried to copy her. Sylva wasn't sure what was going on, but Grandmother sat very straight with a little smile at the corner of her mouth. He never fussed again until it was all over.

I wore a green silk dress that Mama brought me from Paris. "It brings out your eyes," she said after we got it all unwrapped from the tissue paper. "Your papa always said green was your color, and I believe he was right."

I said, "I miss my papa," and Mama said, "So do I, sweetheart." She sat down on the bed and took my hands in hers. Then she turned them over and touched the scars with the tips of her fingers. "How can you ever forgive me, Franny?" she asked. I couldn't say anything, Papa, but I couldn't let go of her hands either. Then she said to me, "Franny, I did meet a gentleman on our journey. He was very kind, and in some ways I was drawn to him, but Franny, I'm not ready for that yet. You and I need time together first."

Then I said back to her, "I'm glad you're home, Mama."